LIZZIE AND CHARLEY
GO TO THE MOVIES

Dyan Sheldon is a children's writer, adult novelist and humorist. Her children's titles include *Leon Loves Bugs*, *He's Not My Dog* and the prequel to this book, *Lizzie and Charley Go Shopping*. She has also written three stories about an alien cat and his human minder, *Harry and Chicken*, *Harry the Explorer* and *Harry's Holiday*, and several picture books, including *The Whales' Song* (winner of the 1991 Kate Greenaway Medal). Among her numerous titles for young adults are *Undercover Angel*, *Undercover Angel Strikes Again*, *Confessions of a Teenage Drama Queen*, *And Baby Makes Two* and *The Boy of My Dreams*. American by birth, Dyan Sheldon lives in north London.

Lizzie and Charley Go to the Movies

DYAN SHELDON

WALKER BOOKS
AND SUBSIDIARIES
LONDON • BOSTON • SYDNEY

First published 2001 by Walker Books Ltd
87 Vauxhall Walk, London SE11 5HJ

2 4 6 8 10 9 7 5 3 1

Text © 2001 Dyan Sheldon
Cover illustration © 2001 Nick Sharratt

This book has been typeset in Plantin

Printed and bound in Great Britain by The Guernsey Press Co. Ltd

British Library Cataloguing in Publication Data:
a catalogue record for this book
is available from the British Library

ISBN 0-7445-5974-X

Contents

Mrs Moscos Convinces Lizzie to Go to the Movies, in Spite of her Sister

Lizzie slammed the back door behind her and threw herself into one of the garden chairs with an angry thump.

"And what's wrong with you today, Lizzie Wesson?" asked the very large tree on the other side of the garden wall. "Your face is longer than a giraffe."

Lizzie looked over. A small figure in baggy jeans, a Greenpeace T-shirt and yellow gardening gloves was sitting in the branches of the tree. It was Lizzie's neighbour, Mrs Moscos. Although sitting in a tree would have been a strange activity for any of Lizzie's other neighbours, it was normal enough for

Mrs Moscos. Mrs Moscos said she came from somewhere in Eastern Europe. She certainly didn't talk like anyone else on Meteor Drive. Everyone in the neighbourhood regarded Mrs Moscos as very eccentric if not actually mad. Not only did she grow fruit and vegetables in her garden instead of flowers like everyone else, but lately she had started decorating the enormous old chestnut in her backyard with hundreds of blue and white fairy lights that shone every night, no matter what the weather. She spent quite a bit of time replacing the bulbs that were always burning out. Which explained what she was doing in the tree.

"Oh, hi, Mrs Moscos," said Lizzie.

"What's the matter?" Mrs Moscos leaned forward so that it looked like just her head was in the tree, smiling down at Lizzie in a slightly disturbing way. "All dressed up and nowhere to go?"

Lizzie had never heard this expression

before, but it was so accurate that she laughed. It was not a happy laugh. Lizzie was all dressed up in her best black trousers and her favourite striped top; and she definitely had nowhere to go. Not any more.

"My mother was meant to take me and Charley for a picnic today," grumbled Lizzie. Charley Desoto was Lizzie's best friend. "But she can't because the pipes are blocked and she has to stay in until the plumber comes."

Mrs Moscos shrugged. "And isn't that just like life?" she asked. "Always full of surprises."

Lizzie didn't like surprises. Not this sort at least. She scowled in a very unattractive way. "But we've been waiting all week for this picnic," she wailed. "My mother promised we could go to the park when it finally stopped raining." She swung her legs back and forth, banging her feet against the chair. "And now she wants us to go to the movies with Allie and Gemma instead." Lizzie made it sound as if going to the movies were a punishment and not a treat.

"And what is the problem with that? I thought you loved the cinema. I've even known you to see the same film more than once." Mrs Moscos shook her head as though the ability to watch the same movie two or three times in a row was the most baffling thing she could imagine.

"Well, I don't love the cinema any more," Lizzie gloomily announced. "Now I think movies are stupid."

"Stupid?" Mrs Moscos cocked an eyebrow. "And what brought about this remarkable change? Was there a blue moon recently that I missed?"

Lizzie kicked her foot against the paving stones, avoiding Mrs Moscos's gaze. Mrs Moscos had very penetrating eyes.

"It's Allie's fault," Lizzie admitted, feeling oddly compelled to tell the truth. "I'm off the movies since Allie got that part in *Our Road*."

Our Road was a popular TV programme about ordinary people. Because it was about ordinary people, the programme used a few real ordinary people each week. Allie Wesson had been in last night's episode. It wasn't a big part. Allie only had one line ("Good morning, miss"), but the way she'd been carrying on since the filming you'd think she was the star.

"Ah," said Mrs Moscos, "I see. We are a little jealous, are we?"

Lizzie scowled even more. "No," she snapped. "We are not a little jealous. We are just very fed up."

In Lizzie's opinion, being on television had made her sister even more full of herself than she usually was – which was quite a great deal. To make matters worse, since the programme aired the phone hadn't stopped ringing with people calling to congratulate Allie and praise her performance. Allie was swanning around as if she'd been nominated for an Academy Award.

"Besides," Lizzie went on grumpily, "Charley and I never have any fun when we go anywhere with Allie. All she does is yell at us and boss us around."

Mrs Moscos unscrewed a bulb from the string of lights and stuffed it into her pocket. "She can't yell and boss you around in the cinema," she pointed out. "Perhaps you should go. You seem rather bored."

Lizzie was considerably more than rather bored. She was bored beyond belief. This was the last day of half-term and she'd had nothing to do the entire week because it had rained every single day. Unless you counted listening to her sister boast about being a film star something to do.

"I'd rather go to school," grumbled Lizzie. "I'd rather go to school and do nothing but maths all day." School and maths were Lizzie's least favourite things in the entire universe.

Mrs Moscos made a sound that was very similar to the one the pipes had made when they got blocked. "You're probably right," she said. "And also I am sure it won't hurt you to miss out on popcorn and fizzy drinks for once."

Lizzie was so wound up about her sister that she'd completely forgotten about the spicy popcorn and the cherry-cola they sold at the cinema. Unlike school and maths, these were two of Lizzie's most favourite things.

"And the chocolates and sweeties too, of course..." added the voice from the tree.

Lizzie sighed. Chocolates and sweeties were two more of her most favourite things.

If Lizzie had been paying attention it might have occurred to her that it was very unusual for Mrs Moscos to encourage her to eat either popcorn or sweets. Just as it was extraordinarily unusual for Mrs Moscos to encourage Lizzie to spend the afternoon in a dark cinema when she could be outdoors. Mrs Moscos didn't believe in things like shopping and watching films; Mrs Moscos believed in having adventures.

But Lizzie, of course, was not really paying

attention. She was too busy thinking about cherry-cola and what a first-class pain in the bum her sister was.

"And of course, we must not forget about your sister's feelings," continued Mrs Moscos. She popped another bulb into her pocket. "I shouldn't think Allie wants to be lumbered with you and Charley all afternoon, either. I imagine she'll be delighted that you don't want to go with her. Younger sisters can be such a burden, can't they?"

It was the word "burden" that did it. Lizzie had an image of her sister, staggering along under an enormous pile of bags and boxes like a mule. She liked the idea of Allie being a mule almost as much as she liked the idea of being a burden to her. Mrs Moscos was right. If Lizzie and Charley stayed at home, Allie would go to the movies and have a wonderful time. Why should Allie have a wonderful time when Lizzie was having a miserable one? Why should Lizzie be the only one to suffer?

"Maybe you're right," mused Lizzie.

"Maybe I should go."

"Oh, no, no, no…" said Mrs Moscos. "You were completely right. Why should you sit in a dark cinema, stuffing your face with popcorn and sweets, when you could be sitting in the garden, watching me change the lights?"

Put that way, it seemed to Lizzie that there really wasn't any choice. She jumped to her feet.

"I'll see you later, Mrs Moscos," she called as she ran into the house. "I've got to ring Charley and tell her we're going to the movies after all."

The Wrong Cinema

"Look at her, will you?" grumbled Lizzie. She pointed to Allie, who was striding along, head held high and smiling as though the street were lined with photographers waiting to take her picture. Lizzie snorted derisively. "She looks ridiculous."

Allie was wearing all the new gear she'd bought with the money she'd earned from saying "Good morning, miss" on national television: platform boots, silk cargo pants and extremely large sunglasses with bright yellow frames.

"I don't know about that," answered Charley, who rather fancied the cargo pants, "but she definitely doesn't look as though she's very burdened, does she?"

This was all too true. Mrs Moscos's sympathy for poor Allie, burdened by her

little sister, had been sadly misplaced. Allie was about as burdened by the presence of Lizzie and Charley as an elephant is burdened by having a butterfly on its back.

"She does seem pretty annoyed, though," Charley continued. "I suppose that's something."

Lizzie's bag swung back and forth as they hurried to keep up with Allie. "No, it isn't. Allie's always annoyed."

But Charley's was an optimistic nature. "Well, maybe she's a better actress than we thought," she suggested. "You know. Maybe she's just acting like she isn't burdened."

Lizzie gave Charley a look. "Trust me," she said sourly, "Allie is not that good an actress."

It wasn't until they reached the bus stop where they were meeting Allie's best friend Gemma that Allie finally spoke to Charley and Lizzie.

"Let's get one thing straight," Allie told them. "The only reason I agreed to take you two along is because Mum made me." She pointed a finger at Lizzie. "And if you don't behave, Lizzie Wesson, I'll make you wish you'd never been born."

"I wish *you'd* never been born," Lizzie muttered under her breath.

Allie heard her. "I mean it," she snarled. She crossed her arms and glared at Lizzie and Charley in a grim and menacing way. "Especially after what happened last time."

The last time Lizzie and Charley went out with Allie and Gemma was several weeks before, when the four of them went shopping together. The memory of that afternoon had vanished from Lizzie's and Charley's minds as completely as a drop of water vanishes from the pavement on a hot and sunny afternoon. Both girls knew that something had happened – something very peculiar – but try as they might they couldn't remember what. Allie, however, was certain she knew exactly what had happened. Lizzie and Charley had gone off and left her and

Gemma waiting for them for nearly two hours.

"Don't worry," said Lizzie sweetly. "We won't lose you. We're sticking to you like glue."

"More like mould," said Allie.

At that moment Gemma came rushing down the street shrieking, "I saw you on telly last night! I saw you on telly last night! You were absolutely brilliant!" at the top of her voice, and Allie moved away before Lizzie had a chance to kick her.

There were several other people waiting for the bus, and all of them stood there for the next seven minutes, listening to Allie and Gemma discuss Allie's role in *Our Road* in the most minute detail.

Lizzie kept yawning and rolling her eyes, but Allie and Gemma were too engrossed in their conversation to notice. At last their bus appeared at the top of the road.

"Thank goodness," muttered Lizzie as she and Charley climbed on board. "I can't wait till we get to the cinema. At least they can't talk during the film."

It was, however, several miles to the cinema and Allie and Gemma could talk on the bus. Non-stop. Apparently Allie was planning to move to Hollywood sometime in the near future and star in a film with Leonardo DiCaprio.

"Yeah," Lizzie whispered to Charley. "*Titanic II*, and Allie plays the ship."

Charley sighed. "I just wish she didn't shout so. She's giving me a headache."

Lizzie made the face of a horse with a fly on its nose – which was meant to be Allie playing the great actor – and said, "It isn't shouting, Charley, you poor fool, it's projecting. Actors have to project."

"I'm going to project you into orbit," Allie informed her, suddenly appearing beside them in the aisle. "Now move it. This is our stop."

Lizzie and Charley jumped up and hurried after the older girls. It wasn't until they were on the pavement that they realized Allie had made a mistake.

"This is the wrong stop," said Lizzie as the bus pulled away from the kerb. "The cinema isn't here."

"Yes it is." Allie pointed left. "It's right up there."

Charley groaned softly.

Lizzie stomped her foot. "But you told Mum we were going to the small cinema near the green."

Allie gave her a pitying look. "And why would I do that? The film we want to see is on here."

Lizzie stomped her foot again. "But the film *we* want to see is on at the other one."

Allie, being a great actor, put on a baby voice. "Oh dear, what a shame," she squeaked. Gemma spluttered with giggles. "I guess you'll have to see something else."

"But you told Mum you'd let us pick!" shrieked Lizzie. "Because we didn't go on our picnic!" This time she stomped both her feet. "You did!" she screamed. "I heard you! Mum heard you! You promised!"

"Lizzie." Charley put a hand on her shoulder. "Lizzie, you can stop now. They've gone."

Blinking, Lizzie looked round. Charley was right. Allie and Gemma, their arms linked, were strolling up the road towards the wrong cinema.

So much for Lizzie's hopes of making her sister unhappy.

"Allie always wins, doesn't she?" grumbled Lizzie.

Charley patted her shoulder. "To tell you the truth, I find it very touching that you even try to beat her."

The Wrong Screen

As soon as they reached the cinema, Allie and Gemma bought their tickets and sauntered inside, leaving Charley and Lizzie to decide which of the five films showing that afternoon they wanted to see.

"There isn't exactly a big choice, is there?" said Lizzie miserably.

Charley's eyes moved up and down the programme listing. "Well, the musical's out for a start."

Apart from the fact that Allie and Gemma had gone to it, Lizzie and Charley didn't like musicals. They didn't feel that people suddenly bursting into song was very realistic.

"The cartoon's out too," said Lizzie. "I'm not sitting in a room full of little kids for the next two hours. They make too much noise."

"Then the thriller's out as well," decided

Charley. "It'll be filled with boys throwing popcorn at each other."

"What about the Western?" Lizzie asked without any real enthusiasm.

Charley pretended to gag. "Ugh! I can't stand cowboy movies. If you ask me, they're even less realistic than musicals."

Lizzie sighed. "Well, I reckon it's *Galaxy at War IV* then. Lizzie and Charley had already seen *Galaxy at War IV* when it first came out, and neither of them was very keen on science fiction either. "There isn't anything else."

"That's all right with me," said Charley. "At least we know how it ends." Her eyes drifted towards the snack bar. "We'd better get our tickets so we have time to get plenty to eat," she advised. "Then we won't get so bored we fall asleep."

All the ticket queues were fairly long, so Lizzie and Charley joined the nearest one. Almost immediately it began to speed up.

"This queue's going very fast," commented Charley. "It usually takes ages."

"Maybe it isn't a person selling the tickets," suggested Lizzie. "Maybe it's a machine."

Charley stood on her toes for a better view of the box office. "That's no machine," she reported. "Unless it's some sort of robot."

Lizzie too peered over the heads in front of them. Behind the ticket window was a small woman wearing an enormous blonde wig that fell in thick tangles, dark glasses the size of ping-pong paddles and an unfashionable blue and white jumpsuit.

Charley noticed the frown on Lizzie's face. "What's wrong?"

Lizzie shrugged. "Nothing. It's just that the woman selling the tickets looks sort of familiar."

"Of course she looks familiar," said Charley dismissively. Charley wasn't really paying attention: she was too busy deciding what she was going to eat. "We've been here hundreds of times, haven't we? We're bound to have seen her before."

Lizzie made a doubtful face. "I think I'd

remember if I'd seen her before," she argued. "I mean, she's pretty memorable, isn't she?"

"What does it matter?" asked Charley as they stepped up to the window. "Let's just get our tickets so we can buy our snacks."

Lizzie opened her mouth to tell the woman what they wanted. But the words "Two for Screen Five" were still in her throat when two tickets were roughly thrust into her hand.

Lizzie blinked in surprise. "Oh," she said.

"Next, please!" cried the woman in a high, almost childish voice.

"But we haven't paid yet!" Lizzie protested.

The enormous sunglasses bobbed in Charley and Lizzie's direction. "Oh yes, you have," squeaked the woman. "Of course you've paid. There are no free seats around here, you know."

Lizzie looked at her hand; her money was gone. She looked at Charley's hand; Charley's money was gone too.

Lizzie gave Charley a puzzled glance, but Charley still wasn't paying attention.

"Come on," said Charley, pulling Lizzie away from the window. "Let's just get some food and find our film."

Getting the food was no problem at all. Finding their film, however, proved a bit trickier.

There was one sign for Screen Five on the swinging doors near the popcorn stand, but as soon as they stepped through them there were no more signs at all, just seemingly endless dark, silent corridors that twisted in all directions.

After several long minutes of walking, Charley wanted to know if Lizzie was sure they were going the right way.

Lizzie, who had no idea which way they were going, sighed. "Of course I'm sure. You saw the sign."

"Yeah, I saw the sign – but that was miles ago." Charley leaned against the wall, catching her breath. "And is it my imagination, or are we going uphill?"

"It's your imagination," answered Lizzie,

although she too was a bit out of breath. "Now come on, will you? We're going to miss the beginning if we don't hurry up."

A little grumpily, the girls trudged on. At last, way down at the end of the corridor, they spied a purple neon sign.

"You see?" Lizzie speeded up. "I told you we were going the right way. That's Screen Five dead ahead."

Charley squinted at the distant light. "No it isn't," said Charley. "It's Screen Six."

"You don't have your glasses on," pointed out Lizzie. "It's definitely Screen Five." She laughed. "Besides, there is no Screen Six, remember?"

Charley, however, was a very stubborn girl. "But there *is* a Screen Six," she insisted. Charley was holding quite a few things in her hands – a large popcorn, a large cola, two bars of chocolate and a packet of jelly beans – but she managed to point with her elbow. "And that's it."

Lizzie opened her mouth to argue, but now

that they were closer she could see that Charley was right. The number over the entrance was a large purple six. Lizzie stared at it in a certain amount of confusion. "But it can't be," she said softly. "There is no Screen Six."

"So now what?" asked Charley. "Should we go back and try to find Screen Five?"

Lizzie glanced at her watch. "The film will have started by then."

"And all the ice in our drinks will have melted," put in Charley.

"That's true." Lizzie looked at the neon purple six, glowing in the darkness, and then back to Charley. "And we'll only spill more of our popcorn."

"That's true too," agreed Charley. "Plus my legs are really beginning to hurt."

Lizzie took a deep breath. "Well," she said. "I guess that's decided it. We'll watch whatever's on in Screen Six."

"But what about the ticket-taker?" asked Charley.

Lizzie looked around, but there was no one to be seen. "What ticket-taker?" she asked.

And with that, Lizzie pushed open the door – and she and Charley stepped inside.

The Wrong Movie

Lizzie and Charley stood very close together at the top of the stairs, staring down at the rows of purple seats and the silver screen that shimmered in the dull light of the room.

"There's no one here," whispered Charley. She sounded a little nervous.

Lizzie, of course, had also noticed the absence of an audience other than themselves. She had never been in an empty cinema before and she found it slightly eerie. But she didn't want Charley to know that she was nervous too, and so, in a bright, loud voice, she said, "Well, that's all right. That means we can sit wherever we want."

They sat in the centre of the centre row. Since it was unlikely that there would be a sudden rush of people to fill up all the empty seats, they put their snacks on the chairs beside them.

Charley's nervousness disappeared with the first handful of jelly beans. "I wonder what film it's going to be," she said as she chewed. "I hope it's something we like."

Lizzie scooped up some popcorn. "I hope it's a comedy. I could do with a laugh."

The lights went down.

"If I had a sister like Allie I'd need more than one laugh," said Charley.

Munching away, Charley and Lizzie started talking about Allie and what a class-A pain she was. They heard a door open. Someone slipped into the row behind them.

"You see?" whispered Lizzie. "Didn't I tell you there was nothing to worry about? Lots of people wait till after the adverts."

"Umph," grunted Charley through a mouthful of chocolate.

Feeling even more relaxed now that they were no longer alone, Lizzie and Charley continued talking through the trailers. Allie and all the things that were wrong with her was such an interesting topic of conversation that they only noticed the movie was starting when a very bright object shot over their heads.

Charley looked at Lizzie. "What was that?"

"Popcorn," answered Lizzie, and turned her eyes to the front of the cinema.

A very black night filled with thousands of shooting stars, rotating planets and swirling balls of gas materialized on the screen. The air crackled and hummed with strange sounds.

"Can you believe it?" whispered Charley. "It's the science fiction film. We came to the right screen after all."

Suddenly they were inside what appeared to be the control room of some sort of spaceship, although it didn't look like the interior of any spaceship Charley and Lizzie had ever seen before. Instead of sophisticated equipment and flashing control panels, there was an old-fashioned cockpit and a cumbersome instrument desk. Besides that, the walls were painted with primitive pictures and symbols, and every spare bit of space was filled with plants and trees.

Lizzie frowned. "This isn't *Galaxy at War IV*," she whispered. The spaceships in *Galaxy at War IV* were all very sleek and technologically advanced, and they certainly didn't feature vegetation. "I don't remember it at all."

There were six humanoids seated in the cockpit. They were dressed in immaculate uniforms of purple and gold and their faces were hidden behind gold helmets. The other six occupants of the craft wore rumpled blue and white uniforms and were sound asleep in string hammocks that were strung between the trees.

"I don't remember it either," answered Charley.

Lizzie was still frowning. There was nothing even vaguely familiar about the creatures in the gold helmets, but she had the strangest sensation that there should be something familiar about them.

"That's probably because all science fiction movies are sort of alike, aren't they?" Charley stuffed a few more jelly beans into her mouth. "Or maybe it's because those blokes in the helmets look a bit like Darth Vader. You're confusing it with *Star Wars*."

A mild, deep voice began to speak:

Centuries of warfare have left the galaxy of Upalala battered and divided. In a desperate attempt to restore peace and order, the Intergalactic Corporation of the Western Alliance has stepped in to force a treaty between the powerful planet of Wei and the guerrilla forces of the small planet of Ganow. The Corporation has called for both sides to put down their arms and meet in a neutral place far from Upalala. It is a historic conference. It is the first time in three millennia that the warring planets have sat down together and the only time that the great rebel leader Flyed will leave the mountains and jungles of Ganow to make a public appearance. At this very moment in time, an ancient Ganowan craft, manned by peacekeepers of the Intergalactic

Corporation, is heading towards the secret site of the meeting with Flyed and his aides safely on board.

Lizzie barely heard the mild, deep voice. She was trying to decide if Charley was right about the film reminding her of *Star Wars* or not. It was true that the helmeted creatures did resemble Darth Vader in a very vague way, but apart from that there didn't seem to be many similarities between the two films. The special effects weren't nearly as good.

"You know," said Lizzie as the deep, mild voice droned on, "I don't think I am confusing it with *Star Wars*."

"Well, then you're mixing it up with *Cosmic Crusaders*," answered Charley. "That starts out a bit like this."

Several more pieces of popcorn sailed past their heads.

Charley yawned. "I just hope it gets a little more exciting," she mumbled through another fistful of jelly beans. "This is dead boring. All they're doing is riding through space."

"And all you are doing is talking," said a voice very near them. "Do try to pay attention, girls. You may be tested on this later."

Lizzie and Charley looked round as several more pieces of popcorn sailed past their heads.

Sitting behind them was the woman who had sold them their tickets. Her golden wig seemed almost to glow in the dark of the cinema.

Lizzie was so surprised that she said the first thing that came into her head. "Excuse me," she said politely, "but are you speaking to us?"

"And who else would I be speaking to?" squeaked the woman. She gestured to the rows of seats surrounding them. "Do you see anyone else in here?"

"Well, no…" answered Lizzie and Charley together, flinching as a cluster of popcorn came so close they thought it was going to hit them. Considering the fact that there was no one else in the cinema, the amount of popcorn hurtling about was becoming quite alarming.

"Precisely. Nor do I. Now do be quiet and watch the film. You don't want to miss anything important. Time will not wait and neither of you yet know which of those men is Flyed."

Although neither Lizzie nor Charley saw him get up, one of the Ganowans suddenly appeared beside the peacekeeper sitting in the captain's seat. The Ganowan was a small man, with long fair hair that fell in thick knots and a shy, almost apologetic smile.

The peacekeeper hadn't seen the man get up and cross the room either. Startled, he jumped in his seat, and immediately started to shout in a strange, though oddly familiar, language.

The ticket-seller kindly translated. "The peacekeeper is demanding to know what he wants," she explained. "He is telling him to go back to his hammock and mind his own business."

"Is that Flyed?" asked Lizzie. He didn't look like much of a great rebel leader to her. He didn't even have a gun.

"What's he saying?" asked Charley.

"It is Flyed," replied the ticket-seller, "and he is apologizing for disturbing the commander, but he senses that they may be off course and would like to see the navigation instruments."

Neither Lizzie nor Charley really needed an interpreter to tell them what the peacekeeper's answer was. He began to shout even more, shaking his fist in the air.

The ticket-seller leaned forward. "He wants to know if Flyed is doubting his ability to fly the ship," she reported. "He wants Flyed to know that he has been specially trained and has won many medals and awards."

Flyed reacted to this outburst as though it

hadn't happened. He remained calm and smiling.

"Flyed says that he does not for one nanosecond doubt the guard's ability to fly the ship," the strange woman continued. "But these old ships can be difficult and unreliable. And he is an expert pilot himself, of course."

The peacekeeper shook and shouted some more. At a look from him, two of the other peacekeepers, their weapons drawn, moved towards Flyed, ready to haul him back to his hammock.

Flyed didn't so much as glance round. He raised one hand and spoke so softly that even if he had been speaking in a language Lizzie and Charley understood it was unlikely that they would have known what he had said.

"Flyed says that it will not be necessary for the men at his back to take hold of him," their companion informed them. "He is sorry he disturbed the captain and will go back to his hammock."

It seemed to Lizzie that Flyed wasn't much of a great rebel leader. Surely a great rebel leader wouldn't go back to his hammock just because someone shouted at him. Surely he'd stand his ground.

"He doesn't act like a great rebel leader, does he?" Lizzie whispered to Charley.

Charley had too many sweets in her mouth to answer, but the woman behind them didn't.

"You are not paying attention," she hissed. "If you were you—"

Unfortunately, she never finished her sentence. At that precise moment the room they were in dropped several metres, as though they were sitting not in a comfortable cinema but on a particularly fast big wheel.

"Good grief!" gasped Charley as cherry-cola sprayed over them.

Lizzie looked round at the woman behind them. "But—" she said.

"*But* is a word used most often by young girls with indecisive minds," the ticket-seller told her with a certain amount of coolness. "Now do try to pay attention. You're not going to be of much assistance if you don't know what's happening, are you?"

"Assistance?" Lizzie repeated. Some distant memory was trying to crawl out from the depths of her mind. Some distant memory associated with assistance. "What sort of assistance?"

It was then that Charley screamed.

"Oh my gosh! Lizzie, look! It's…" Charley paused, searching for a name she had forgotten she knew. "Why, it's Louis Wu! Lizzie, look! It's Louis Wu!"

The distant memory finally reached the surface of Lizzie's brain. Incredible as it seemed, Lizzie had totally forgotten about Louis Wu, but now it all came back to her in a rush. She remembered the silver sands of the planet Wei, and the Wei soldiers in their black capes. She remembered that Louis Wu was the exceedingly clever if exceedingly unscrupulous ruler of Wei. And she remembered why she and Charley were late meeting Allie and Gemma the last time the four of them went out together: she and Charley were helping to stop Louis Wu from taking over the Earth.

Lizzie turned back to the film. The scene on the screen had changed. Instead of the spaceship she was looking at a large auditorium. At one end was a row of tables with a speaker's platform in the centre. As Charley said, standing on the platform was Louis Wu. In front of him was a pack of reporters with transmission equipment recording his every word. Louis Wu was telling them about the peace conference.

The mild voice of the narrator began to speak again:

As ruler of Wei and its many colonies, Louis Wu thanks the Intergalactic Corporation for this opportunity to come to an agreement with the warriors of Ganow. He hopes this means that the millennia of terrorism and rebellion have finally come to an end, and that both sides will go on to

prosper and thrive. Louis Wu assures the galaxy
of Upalala that he eagerly awaits the arrival of
Flyed and hopes that this time the great rebel
leader doesn't change his mind about taking part
in the peace process, as he has always done in the
past. Despite the enthusiasm with which he
embraces the possibility of an end to the warfare,
Louis Wu feels he must make it clear that should
Flyed fail to turn up for the conference within the
hour, he, as leader of Wei, will have no choice
but to consider it an act of aggression – and to
retaliate in kind. "It is up to Flyed," says Louis
Wu. "Our future is in his hands."

Lizzie and Charley looked at each other. A
new thought had occurred to both of them.

"You don't think that's Mrs Moscos behind
us, do you?" asked Charley in her softest
voice.

Before Lizzie could answer a hand fell on
each of their shoulders.

"How good of you to at last switch on your
brains," said Mrs Moscos in her own voice,
which was a lot more sarcastic than the voice

she'd been using. "Now, if you would be so kind as to hold on tightly. I believe that we are about to make a landing. We must prepare ourselves to move like light, if not a little faster."

"Land?" Lizzie laughed. "How can we land? We're in a cinema."

"Lizzie—" said Charley.

Now that she knew the strange ticket-seller was really Mrs Moscos, Lizzie felt a little annoyed. "And quite frankly, Mrs Moscos," she went on, "I do think that you owe us an explanation. What do you mean sneaking up on us like that?"

"Lizzie—" said Charley.

"And why are you wearing that wig and those glasses?"

"Lizzie!" roared Charley. "Lizzie, for heaven's sake, shut up and look!"

There was an urgency in Charley's voice that finally made Lizzie do as she was told. She shut up and looked.

While Lizzie wasn't watching, the walls of

the cinema had disappeared. Which meant that it was now obvious that the small whitish objects whizzing past them weren't popcorn at all. They were meteorites.

And, because the walls of the cinema had disappeared, the floor had also disappeared, as had the comfortable seats and the screen itself.

Instead of being in the centre of the centre row of the cinema, they were in a glass bubble attached to the side of the spaceship carrying the great rebel leader Flyed to the signing of the peace treaty. They weren't watching a film at all; they were watching what was happening through the ship's television system.

"Didn't I tell you we shouldn't go into Screen Six?" wailed Charley. "Didn't I tell you it was a mistake? But oh no, you always have to have things your way."

As surprised as she was to find herself in a bubble attached to a spaceship, Lizzie was even more surprised to have Charley turn on her like that. Surprised and hurt. It seemed to Lizzie that she always got the blame for everything. It really wasn't fair.

"You said no such thing!" Lizzie shouted back. "You said we might as well come in here!"

Mrs Moscos clapped her hands. "Girls! Try to remember that you come from a species that is supposed to be intelligent and act accordingly."

Lizzie was prevented from replying because the ship suddenly hit something extremely hard, which sent all three of them flying in different directions.

"Ah," said Mrs Moscos, straightening her wig and her glasses. "What a surprise: an unscheduled stop."

Out of the Cinema and onto the Asteroid

....

After they were sure they hadn't broken anything in the landing, Lizzie and Charley sat up, rubbing their elbows and warily looking around.

Beyond the clear walls of the cargo bubble they could see large and craggy formations of pink and orange rocks beneath a green and violet sky.

"Gosh," said Charley in almost a whisper. "Where are we?"

"Well, it isn't Earth," said Lizzie.

Mrs Moscos got to her feet. "No," she said, "it definitely isn't Earth." She smoothed out her jumpsuit and readjusted her wig. "Nor, you will not be surprised to hear, is it the neutral planet where the peace conference is being held. It is an obscure, uncharted asteroid in the tail of a forgotten galaxy."

"So what happened?" asked Lizzie. "Did we crash?"

If Lizzie had been the sort of person who thinks ahead, she might have worried about getting off the uncharted asteroid in the tail of a forgotten galaxy, but she wasn't. So instead she found the idea of crashing in a spaceship on an uncharted asteroid rather exciting.

"In a manner of speaking." Mrs Moscos started rummaging through her hair. "But not in the accidental manner of speaking, you understand."

Charley, who found the idea of crashing in a spaceship considerably less exciting than Lizzie did, was worried. "You mean the Corporation peacekeepers crashed the ship on purpose? Why would they do a thing like that?"

Mrs Moscos pulled several unwanted objects out of her wig and tossed them over her shoulder. "Because they are not Corporation peacekeepers, why else?"

"Then who are they?" asked Charley.

Lizzie's eyes widened as she finally realized why the creatures in purple and gold had seemed familiar. "They're Wei soldiers."

Mrs Moscos nodded approvingly, causing a few more articles to fall from her hair. "Precisely," she said. "They are Wei soldiers. Though in disguise, of course."

Because she often didn't pay attention, Lizzie was often confused. The odd thing was that now, when she was paying very close attention, she was still confused. "But what about the peace conference?"

"Peace conference?" Mrs Moscos's head bobbed as if it were on a spring and several small light bulbs fell to the ground. "Lizzie Wesson, did you learn nothing from our last encounter with Louis Wu? Nothing at all?"

It struck Lizzie as totally unfair that even on an uncharted asteroid in a galaxy the universe had forgotten she was still being picked on. "Of course I did," she said warmly. Among other things, she'd learned to stay out of Happy Burger. "I—"

"Well then, you must know that a Wei never tells the truth when a Wei can lie," snapped Mrs Moscos. "Not for half a nanosecond did Louis Wu ever intend to make peace with the Ganowans. After several thousand years of fighting, Louis Wu has finally realized that the only way he will ever defeat the Ganowans is if he first eliminates their leader. Which is why no one except Flyed's own army has ever seen him. He has been very careful not to put himself in a position where he could be harmed or abducted. Not only has he made no public appearances, but there are no photographs or electronic images of him either."

"Gosh," said Charley. "So they used the peace conference as an excuse to get Flyed away from his army?"

Mrs Moscos finally found what she was looking for – a small screwdriver – and slipped it into the pocket of her jumpsuit. "Precisely. It is a simple plan, but it is nonetheless an effective one."

"Well, it doesn't seem all that effective to me," grumbled Lizzie. "How are the Weis going to get back to their planet if they've crashed their ship?" It struck her that this was a very good question.

But it didn't strike Mrs Moscos the same way. "Your concern about the fate of the Weis is very touching," said Mrs Moscos, "but you need not worry. Louis Wu has thought of that." She gave Lizzie a sour smile. "There is a Wei ship waiting nearby to take them home."

"But what about Flyed?" asked Lizzie. "What are they going to do? Just leave him here?"

The blonde wig shook back and forth. "Oh nononono ... Louis Wu will use Flyed's failure to attend the peace conference as an excuse for renewing his war with Ganow. Without a leader, the Ganowans can be easily defeated. It is crucial, therefore, that Flyed dies. If he lives, he will eventually find his way home again and ruin Louis Wu's plan."

Charley looked shocked. "You don't mean they're going to kill Flyed?"

"Wow!" breathed Lizzie. "Murder!" Not only had she never crashed in a spaceship before, she had never been this close to a murder before either.

"I am sorry to disappoint you girls," said Mrs Moscos, hurriedly stuffing all the things she had thrown out of her hair back into it. "It is true that the Weis intend to lure Flyed and his men outside on one pretext or another, and it is also true that once outside they will be ambushed by the Wei troops that have come with the rescue ship." She smirked. "But what one plans in life is not always what happens, as I'm sure even you must know by now. There will be no murder today – not if I have anything to do with it."

"You mean you're going to stop the Weis from killing Flyed?"

Mrs Moscos slung her bag over her shoulder. "Not I, Lizzie Wesson," she said.

"We. Perhaps I should have been more careful using the memory eraser on your delicate human mind. You should have remembered that much by now. We. When you are dealing with someone like Louis Wu it is always good to have reinforcements." She sighed. "No matter how unlikely they may be."

Charley looked nervously at Lizzie. Charley wasn't too keen on the idea of being Mrs Moscos's reinforcements. "But how?" she fretted. "How can we take on the Wei army all on our own?"

"That's right," chimed in Lizzie. "We're only little girls. And you're—" She was about to say, "And you're just an old lady with a screwdriver" but – perhaps fortunately – Mrs Moscos cut her off.

"I'm the one with the plan, that's who I am," said Mrs Moscos. The wall she was standing beside suddenly opened and she strode through.

"Mrs Moscos!" cried Lizzie. "Mrs Moscos,

what about us? You can't just leave us here like this."

Mrs Moscos stopped and looked over her shoulder. "I wasn't leaving you anywhere," she said a little sharply. "I was expecting you to follow me."

Charley grabbed Lizzie's hand. "But Mrs Moscos," said Charley. "Where are we going?"

"I'll give you a hint," Mrs Moscos called back. "We're not going for more popcorn."

Mrs Moscos Has a Plan

Lizzie and Charley followed Mrs Moscos through the wall of the spaceship and into a fuse cupboard that opened into the control room.

"So," said Mrs Moscos, "if you are both standing comfortably, I will quickly tell you my plan."

"Well, I don't know about comfortable," mumbled Lizzie.

It was a very narrow cupboard. Not only were the hairs of Mrs Moscos's wig tickling her nose, but every time Lizzie moved she hit something.

"Good," declared Mrs Moscos, as though Lizzie had said that she had never been more comfortable in her life. "Now listen very carefully. There is no time for me to say everything twice."

Since there wasn't much else to do in the cupboard, Lizzie and Charley listened very carefully.

Mrs Moscos's plan was simple in the extreme. All they had to do was make sure that Flyed didn't leave the ship; overpower the Wei soldiers; find the rescue ship; disarm its guards; and take Flyed home.

"Easy-peasy, as your species likes to say," concluded Mrs Moscos with a smile.

Neither Lizzie nor Charley smiled back. Mrs Moscos's plan contained too much overpowering and disarming of Wei soldiers to seem easy-peasy to either of them.

"You can't be serious," protested Charley. "I can't overpower a Wei soldier. I'm not very good at sport."

It struck Lizzie that even an Olympic athlete might have a bit of trouble disarming a troop of Wei soldiers, and she said as much to Mrs Moscos.

Mrs Moscos, as always, was unsympathetic. "You really must learn not to be so negative,

Lizzie Wesson," she admonished. She removed a small blue glass from the depths of her wig and put it against the wall. "A positive attitude is very important in situations such as this."

"All right," said Lizzie. "I'm positive we can't take on the Wei army and win."

Mrs Moscos gave her a look that would freeze yoghurt. "I need complete quiet for this," she said. She squashed her wig against the glass. "You can't expect me to hear what's going on in the control room with you blathering in my ear."

Lizzie hadn't expected any such thing, but she wisely decided not to argue. After several seconds of silence, however, she risked another question.

"Well?" she whispered impatiently. "What are they saying?"

"They are suggesting to Flyed that they form a search party to explore the asteroid while the engineer repairs the communication network."

"And what's Flyed saying?" asked Charley.

Mrs Moscos pursed her lips. "He's saying that that occurs to him as an excellent idea."

"That's not good, is it?" asked Charley.

"All things contain both good and bad," answered Mrs Moscos. "It is bad because if Flyed leaves the ship we will have no chance of saving him. But it is good because our moment to act has arrived."

Lizzie concentrated on being positive. There was probably nothing to worry about. It stood to reason that Mrs Moscos must have a secret weapon of some kind – or perhaps even several – that she and Charley knew nothing about.

"So what do we do?" asked Lizzie. "Do you have guns and grenades?"

"Oh, I have something much better than guns and grenades," replied Mrs Moscos. "If you would be good enough to go into my pocket and retrieve my screwdriver – I'm afraid I can't reach it myself."

"Your screwdriver?" Lizzie's voice was

slightly shrill with disbelief. "We're going to attack the Weis with a screwdriver?"

"Oh how I wish I hadn't let you talk me into going into Screen Six," moaned Charley.

"Do be quiet the two of you," ordered Mrs Moscos. "Naturally we are not going to attack anyone with a screwdriver. We are going to use it to switch off the power. Surprise will be on our side. In the confusion and darkness we will be able to disarm the soldiers and escape with Flyed."

Lizzie had another question. "But how will we be able to tell the soldiers from the Ganowans in the dark?"

Mrs Moscos sighed, as though of all the ridiculous questions Lizzie had ever asked her, this was the most ridiculous.

"Because the Ganowans glow in the dark, of course."

Charley said, "They do?" She sounded quite surprised.

"It's because of their energy," Mrs Moscos explained. "It is because of the way they use their minds. Rather than using only a fraction of their brains – as your species does – the Ganowans use both sides to their full power. It makes them rather special."

"And is that why Louis Wu has never defeated the Ganowans?" asked Lizzie. "Because they're so special?"

"Precisely. The Ganowans are, as you humans say, a thorn in the side."

"In the side of what?" asked Charley.

Mrs Moscos sighed. "In the side of Louis Wu's plans for intergalactic conquest. You see, Ganow is not only a magnificent planet, it is an unspoilt one as well. That is because the Ganowans, though brilliant scientists, have chosen a very unscientific lifestyle."

"I still don't understand why Louis Wu wants Ganow so much," said Lizzie.

"Ah, well..." Mrs Moscos's voice held a touch of pride. "I am afraid that is the fault of you and I. Since we ruined his plan to take over the Earth, he has become more determined than ever to capture Ganow. They are, in many ways, twin planets, you see. Although Ganow, of course, is in much better condition."

"But if the Ganowans are so unscientific, why haven't the Weis been able to beat them?"

"They have the technology, Lizzie Wesson, but they choose not to use it. They use their energy instead. Now let's have a little more action and less talk. Hand me the screwdriver, please."

Mrs Moscos took the screwdriver from Lizzie's hand and removed a small panel from the wall of fuses and meters. Behind the panel was a hole. Mrs Moscos jammed the screwdriver into the hole.

There was a small explosion of blue light and the smell of something burning. And then everything went extremely still and dark.

"Quick as gluons!" hissed Mrs Moscos. She pulled a torch from her hair and turned it on. "Follow me."

And, in accordance with her habit of opening walls, Mrs Moscos gave a shove to one side of the cupboard and disappeared.

Plan B

....

Lizzie and Charley would have been perfectly happy to stay in the fuse cupboard, but they had been so squashed together that when Mrs Moscos left both girls fell through the opening after her.

Although the light from Mrs Moscos's torch was dim, Lizzie and Charley could see immediately that, with the exception of Mrs Moscos, the room was empty.

"Where is everyone?" whispered Lizzie.

Mrs Moscos, who was busily scuttling around the control room searching for something, didn't look over. "Well, they're not here, are they?" she snapped.

"But why not?" Charley's voice wobbled. "You said we'd be able to overtake them. You said surprise would be on our side."

Mrs Moscos's sigh was as sour as a fart. "It

just goes to show you that there is nothing you can rely on in this universe, doesn't it?" She dived behind a tree. "Not even the stupidity of Wei soldiers can be depended on. They must have suspected a trap and escaped through the emergency hatch as soon as the power went off."

"But what about the Ganowans?" pressed Lizzie. "What happened to them?"

Even in the limited light, Lizzie could see the look of irritation on Mrs Moscos's face.

"I can't be certain, of course – they may all have needed to use the toilet – but my guess would be that the Weis took them with them."

"So by now they've been ambushed by the extra soldiers…" finished Charley gloomily.

Lizzie didn't share Charley's gloom. In fact, this struck her as good news. If the Ganowans had already been ambushed, then there was nothing left for them to do. "So that means we can go home," she said.

Mrs Moscos sighed again. "Nothing is as

simple as you would like it to be," she informed Lizzie from under a hammock. "You will remember, of course, that Flyed was concerned that the ship was off course right from the start."

Lizzie and Charley, who remembered this only vaguely, both nodded.

"And, being rational beings, you will have therefore deduced that he was aware that a trap had been set for him."

"Right," mumbled Charley and Lizzie, who had deduced no such thing.

Mrs Moscos was now crawling along the floor, shining her torch into the smallest gaps. "It therefore stands to reason that Flyed has not allowed himself to be captured by the Weis," she continued. "He will most certainly have escaped."

"Then where is he?" asked Lizzie and Charley together.

Mrs Moscos's head rose above the control console as she got back on her feet. "I'm afraid that that is something I do not at the moment know." She waved her torch from one side of the room to another. "He does not seem to be here."

"So now what do we do?" asked Charley.

"I suggest we move on to Plan B," said Mrs Moscos. And with that she suddenly sat down on the nearest chair.

Several very long minutes passed very slowly.

Lizzie knew that Mrs Moscos didn't like to be asked annoying questions. She also knew that Mrs Moscos considered even the most reasonable question put to her by Lizzie to be annoying. But patience was not one of Lizzie Wesson's virtues and eventually she couldn't stand the suspense any more.

"Mrs Moscos," said Lizzie very gently. "Mrs Moscos, if you have a Plan B, don't you think we should be putting it into action, instead of sitting here in the dark doing nothing?"

Although the light from the torch was feeble, Lizzie could still see the look of annoyance on her neighbour's face.

"Perhaps you are doing nothing," answered Mrs Moscos. "I myself am doing quite a lot."

"Really?" Lizzie couldn't hide her surprise. "What are you doing?"

"I am waiting."

"Waiting…" echoed Charley.

"Waiting…" repeated Mrs Moscos.

Lizzie was wondering exactly what it was Mrs Moscos was waiting for when her question was answered as though she had asked it out loud.

"Waiting for me," said a gentle voice that did not belong to Mrs Moscos.

Lizzie and Charley turned round. Stepping through the hole in the wall behind them was the great rebel leader Flyed, biting into what looked remarkably like a jelly bean.

"This is very good," said Flyed, chewing thoughtfully. He looked hopefully at Lizzie and Charley. "Do you have any more?"

Charley stammered with confusion. "W– well, no … I – I'm afraid I spilled them—"

"And I am afraid there is no time for chit-chat," interrupted Mrs Moscos. The ground beneath the spacecraft began to tremble. She stood up and looked out the window. "Since the so-called Corporation peacekeepers and a very large percentage of the Wei army are coming our way, it's probably time you disguised yourself," she called over her shoulder to Flyed. "I see they've brought the shield gun."

Lizzie didn't really want to ask what a shield gun was, but she felt that someone had to. "What's a shield gun?"

"It is exactly what it sounds like," said Mrs Moscos, crossing the room to stand beside them. "It creates an invisible shield around whatever it is fired at – a spaceship, for example – so that no one can enter or leave."

"That's really not good news, is it?" asked Charley.

"Not so that one would actually notice, no," agreed Mrs Moscos. "Which is why we must act quickly. I will hurry to Ganow to tell

Flyed's army what has happened and to get reinforcements."

"What about us?" asked Lizzie. "You're not leaving us here on our own, are you?"

"Of course not. You two shall escape from the ship and take Flyed with you. You must get him to the peace conference before the deadline is up."

Charley gasped. "But he's gone!"

Lizize looked behind them, but Charley was right: Flyed was no longer there.

"Of course he's not gone," said Mrs Moscos. "He has cleverly disguised himself, that is all."

Lizzie couldn't see anything that might be a great rebel leader in disguise. "Disguised himself as what?"

Mrs Moscos scooped something from her shoulder with one finger and held it out to Lizzie. "Here."

Perched on Mrs Moscos's fingertip was a small blue and white butterfly.

"That's Flyed?" Lizzie couldn't help feeling

sceptical. It seemed to her that if a great rebel leader was going to turn himself into something else he would turn himself into something ferocious like a lion, not into a helpless butterfly.

"We do not have time for me to tell you everything more than once," said Mrs Moscos, thrusting the butterfly at her. "And do pay attention, Lizzie Wesson. You must get Flyed to the peace conference before Louis Wu can declare war on Ganow. Do you understand?"

"Well, sort of..." Lizzie hesitated. She didn't like to admit that there were a few small details she wasn't quite sure of, because she didn't want to be snapped at by Mrs Moscos again.

"I don't," said Charley. "How are we meant to get out of here? How are we meant to find the conference?"

In answer, Mrs Moscos dug into her hair again and came out with a small, neon-purple object. "You are going through this door."

She threw the object at the wall. A door immediately appeared with a lit purple EXIT sign above it.

"But that's like the sign in the cinema," said Charley.

"Precisely." Mrs Moscos had already opened another door in the floor and was climbing into it. "So you should have no difficulty knowing what to do."

"But Mrs Moscos," said Lizzie as the mass of hair began to disappear, "you haven't told us how we're going to find the conference."

"Don't worry!" Mrs Moscos called back to them. Her voice already sounded very far away. "Just keep going through the doors."

"Doors?" shouted Lizzie. "Mrs Moscos, what doors?"

"The doors through space and time, of course. Every moment has an exit, you know. But not everyone can find them."

"Well, thank goodness she answered that question," muttered Charley.

Lizzie continued to stare through the hole

in the floor. "But Mrs Moscos—"

Mrs Moscos's voice was very, very far away now. "Stay close to Flyed," it said. "He's very good at locating the doors. I will find you, if you survive."

Not Quite Lost in Space

....

Mrs Moscos's voice hung in the air as the floor of the spaceship closed over her head. *I will find you if you survive ... if you survive...*

"I don't like the sound of that," whispered Charley. She didn't think much of the word "if". It had only two letters, but it still seemed to her an extremely large word. "If we survive? What does she mean *if*?"

Lizzie, however, had rushed to the window, hoping to catch a last glimpse of Mrs Moscos. What she had more than a glimpse of was several Wei soldiers in the black and silver capes she remembered all too well. They were pointing a very large and impressive-looking gun at the Ganowan craft.

"It means that if we don't get out of that door right away we definitely won't survive," replied Lizzie, and grabbing hold of Charley she hurried towards the purple EXIT sign.

For once, not thinking too much was an advantage, because if Lizzie had stopped to think about the consequences of going through a door that didn't exist, she probably wouldn't have gone. Instead, she turned the handle and pulled Charley through only seconds before the invisible shield sealed the spacecraft tight.

The door slammed behind them and the girls leaned against it, catching their breath. A delicate blue light surrounded them like a cocoon.

"Whew…" gasped Lizzie. "That was close. Thank goodness we got out of there in time."

Charley, however, was still thinking about the word "if". She said, "Um…"

Lizzie tried to peer through the blue light, but there was nothing to be seen. "I guess this must be a special hideout. You know, where we'll be safe until Mrs Moscos comes back for us."

"*If* she comes back," said Charley.

Lizzie looked down at her finger. The blue and white butterfly was still there. "At least Flyed seems all right." It was a little hard to tell with butterflies.

This time Charley said, "Oh ... the light's starting to evaporate."

Lizzie was only half listening. She leaned her head towards the small blue and white creature on her hand. "You are all right, aren't you?" she asked.

Charley tugged on her arm. "Lizzie! Lizzie, I don't think Flyed is our most important problem at the moment."

Lizzie disagreed. Mrs Moscos had given her Flyed to protect and she was going to do the best job she could. "If we survive and Flyed doesn't it won't make any difference, because Mrs Moscos will kill us," she replied. Lizzie tilted her head for a better look at the great rebel leader. Not so much as an antenna twitched. He seemed to be asleep.

Considering what she said next, Charley's voice was really quite calm. "Lizzie," she said.

Her fingers dug into Lizzie's arm. "Lizzie, we're not alone."

Lizzie tore her eyes from Flyed. Now that the blue light had disappeared, she saw that they were in some sort of lift. The doors of the lift were open. Charley was right: they were definitely not alone.

Beyond the doorway of the lift stretched the command room of an enormous starship, manned by a crew of beings from dozens of different planets wearing the red and green uniform of the Intergalactic Star Force. Every one of them was staring at Lizzie and Charley.

This time, Lizzie knew exactly why everything seemed so familiar: she had seen this movie before.

"Good grief..." she breathed. "We're in *Galaxy at War IV.*"

Charley reached out and took hold of Lizzie's hand, the one that had no butterfly sleeping on it. "It certainly looks like it, doesn't it?" she whispered.

"Who in the universe is that?" shouted Allen Smith, captain of the starship. "What are those two girls doing here?"

Having seen all four *Galaxy at War* films, Lizzie and Charley knew that Captain Smith had a very short temper. They were going to have to say something before he pushed a button and beamed them somewhere else.

"We can explain," they said together. "We were on this asteroid – this uncharted asteroid – and we were surrounded by Wei soldiers—"

"Why?" bawled the captain. "Why what?"

"No, Wei," said Lizzie. "Wei is the planet ruled by Louis Wu."

"Who?" asked the captain.

MT9, the co-captain, said, "What planet Wei? There's no planet named Wei."

"Oh, but there is!" exclaimed Charley. "We've been there. It has silver sand and this amazing city…"

Captain Smith, however, wasn't listening. He turned to Eliada, the engineer. "Who are these girls?" he demanded. "What are they doing here?"

Lizzie took a deep breath and started to explain again. "We were on this uncharted asteroid and the Wei army—"

"There is no Wei army!" shouted Captain Smith. "I should know. I've patrolled these galaxies for over twenty years – and I've never heard of Wei."

"Captain!" It was Garpo, the navigator. He was looking at the vision screen. "Captain! Enemy warship approaching. It is armed and ready to fire."

The crew all turned towards the vision screen with cries of alarm. Lizzie and Charley turned too. Rapidly approaching from behind was a black and silver spacecraft with flashing violet lights.

"And who in tarnation is that?" roared Captain Smith. "I've never seen a ship like that before."

Charley squeezed Lizzie's hand.

"That," said Lizzie, "is the Wei army."

"Well, part of it," put in Charley.

Everyone looked at Lizzie and Charley.

Captain Smith stood up. "*That* is the Wei army?" He pointed at the ship that was moving towards them at an extremely fast speed. "What are they doing chasing us?"

It seemed to Lizzie that they had been very lucky to land in the Star Force ship. If this wasn't protection she didn't know what was. This knowledge made her brave enough to tell the truth.

"Well, actually, they probably aren't chasing you." She carefully raised her right hand. "You see this butterfly?"

"Butterfly?" Captain Smith's face was so red Lizzie was afraid he might choke. "We're being chased by a hostile warship and you're talking about butterflies?" He banged his fist on the desk. "Don't think you can trick me, young lady. That ship is chasing you!"

"Only sort of," said Charley. "Because of the butterfly."

Captain Smith looked as if he meant to

start screaming again, but before he could the ship's sound system crackled and a voice that was clearly used to being obeyed filled the air. "This is the Wei warship! We want the girls from Earth! We saw them leave the Ganowan vessel – and we know they know where Flyed is. Hand them over or we will blast you into the next galaxy."

Captain Smith's eyes darted from Lizzie to Charley and back again. "What is this?" he demanded. "Some kind of a joke? Did our producer put you up to this?"

Before either Lizzie or Charley could answer, there was a shrill whine and several Wei rockets flew past the starship, causing it to rock back and forth and shattering one of the instrument panels.

"Jumping juggernauts!" shrieked the navigator. "They're firing at us!"

This information threw the rest of the crew into a considerable amount of panic.

"Now what are we meant to do?" moaned the navigator.

Captain Smith, however, was not fleet commander for nothing. He knew exactly what to do. "Beam them out of here!" he ordered. "If they go, that ship will go too."

Eliada obediently pushed a button. The air around Lizzie and Charley began to tingle and sparkle with particles of light.

"Oh, no," groaned Charley, "we're going to be beamed into deepest space. How are we going to find one of Mrs Moscos's doors in deepest space?"

Lizzie, however, wasn't paying the slightest bit of attention to Charley. Flyed had chosen that moment to wake up. A wing brushed Lizzie's skin as he rose in the air.

"Flyed!" gasped Lizzie. "Flyed, what are you doing?"

"He seems to be leaving," said Charley.

Flyed fluttered delicately above Lizzie's hand for a second, and then, just as she reached out to catch him, he shot into the command room, more like a bullet than a butterfly.

"Flyed! Come back!" shouted Lizzie, and hurled herself after him through the sparkling curtain of light.

Charley could think of only one thing that was worse than being beamed into deepest space – and that was being beamed into deepest space on her own. "Don't leave me here!" she shrieked. "Lizzie, wait for me!"

The ship rocked as another Wei missile exploded nearby.

The crew started shouting again, but none louder than Captain Smith. "Get those children out!" he roared. "Get them out now!"

Several creatures brandishing laser guns rushed off in pursuit of Charley and Lizzie.

The command room was large and there were half a dozen doors through which one could leave. Flyed didn't so much as twitch his antennae at any of them. Moving so fast that he looked like a streak of blue light, he headed straight for the vision screen. And then he disappeared.

"Flyed!" shouted Lizzie. "Flyed, come back!"

Behind her she could hear the heavy footsteps of the starship crew.

Charley heard them too. "He's gone!" she shrieked. "He's gone and we're trapped. Oh, Lizzie, what'll we do?"

For once in her life, Lizzie felt she knew exactly what to do. "We go through the vision screen."

This wasn't the answer Charley had been hoping for. "We do what? We go through what?"

"That has to be where Flyed went," reasoned Lizzie. "Just look at the screen."

Charley's fingers dug into Lizzie's arm. "I have looked. There's nothing there but the Wei warship."

"And stars," said Lizzie. "Look at the stars."

It was true that most of the vision screen was filled with the image of the Wei warship, but it was also true that surrounding the ship were thousands of stars.

"So what?" snapped Charley. "We're in a starship. We're not going to see parrots out the window, are we?"

Lizzie pointed to a tiny constellation in one corner of the screen. "Look closely," she urged.

The tiny constellation in the corner of the screen wasn't the Big Dipper or Orion's Belt. It wasn't the Crab of Cancer or the Twins of Gemini either.

"Why, it's a butterfly!" gasped Charley. A butterfly outlined by blue and white stars.

Charley might still have been a little reluctant to throw herself at the vision screen, but at that very moment a hand clamped down on her shoulder and another hand clamped down on Lizzie's.

"Well done!" boomed the voice of Captain Smith. "Take them out. I want them out of here as of two minutes ago."

Lizzie grabbed Charley's hand. "Ready?" she whispered.

Charley gave the slightest of nods.

And then, much to the surprise of everyone else in the command room, they threw themselves at the butterfly of stars on the screen.

"Now what are they doing?" barked Captain Smith. But even as he spoke there was a sudden whoosh and the girls disappeared.

Charley's disembodied voice lingered in the space where they had been less than a second before.

"Now look what you've done, Lizzie Wesson," it said.

Another Scene Change

Lizzie, Charley and the great rebel leader
Flyed all fell through the stars, landing on a
hillside with a gentle bump.

"Well, this is better," said Charley. She
almost laughed with relief. "This is much
better."

Lizzie checked to make sure that the small
blue and white butterfly on her hand was all
right and then looked around. Charley was
right: it was much better. Instead of being
billions of light-years in deepest space, they
were in an incredibly green field, dotted with
wild flowers in every colour of the rainbow.
Above them the sky was an equally incredible
shade of blue and the sun so round and
yellow it looked like a ball. Happy music was
playing and the birds were singing.

"This is brilliant!" declared Lizzie. "There

isn't a Wei warship in sight." She smiled at Flyed, even though he seemed to have dozed off again. "What a clever butterfly to bring us here," she declared.

Charley sniffed. "Gosh, it smells like a garden centre." She sniffed again, and wrinkled her nose. "Or a perfume counter."

"It must be some sort of park." Lizzie leaned back with her hands behind her head. "I reckon we should just stay here until Mrs Moscos turns up," she said sleepily. It had been a very long afternoon and she was feeling tired.

"Do you think it's almost teatime?" asked Charley. Her stomach growled. It had been a long afternoon for Charley too.

"I don't know…"

Charley also lay back in the grass, but she was too hungry to feel sleepy. "All that food…" she groaned. "I left half my popcorn and a whole chocolate bar in the cinema."

"It's so peaceful here, isn't it?" asked Lizzie. A pink and yellow cloud hovered over the opposite hill.

"And half a packet of jelly beans..."

Lizzie's eyes were slowly closing, but since she didn't want Mrs Moscos to find her asleep when she finally arrived she made an effort to stay awake. "You know, it almost looks as if the sun's wearing dark glasses – and smiling..." mused Lizzie.

"I'm feeling really peckish," said Charley. "I could do with those jelly beans right now."

"And look at those rabbits..." Lizzie felt that she must be dreaming, even though she thought she was awake. "They look like they're wearing clothes and carrying picnic hampers."

"You don't suppose they have any chocolate eggs with them, do you?" asked Charley, who was still paying more attention to her stomach than she was to Lizzie.

"And look at that," Lizzie went on. "Another rabbit has just landed in a small red plane."

"I think I like Creme Eggs best," Charley confided. "Or caramel..."

But Lizzie wasn't listening to Charley. She was listening to her own words running through her head. Smiling suns ... picnicking rabbits ... Lizzie's eyes snapped open. A small red plane with a rabbit at the controls? She sat up.

"Charley" – Lizzie shook her by the hand – "Charley, those aren't rabbits. They're Wabbits."

"Wabbits?" Charley's voice was soft with drowsiness. "Milk chocolate or plain?"

"No, Wabbits!" Lizzie was shouting now. "Wabbits, Charley, Wabbits!"

The Wabbits was one of the most popular cartoon series in children's television history and had just been made into a film.

"We're not in a peaceful field at all," shrieked Lizzie. "We're in another movie! We're in the cartoon!"

"Cartoon?" Charley sat bolt upright. "Gosh..." Her eyes moved from the blue sky and the green grass to the rabbit-like animals spreading a tablecloth over the ground.

"There's Wanda and Wilbur Wabbit – and that's Uncle Buck in the plane. That plane's his pride and joy." Wide awake with shock, she turned to Lizzie. "We are in the cartoon."

Lizzie rolled her eyes. "How nice of you to finally join me, Charlene. What do you think I've been trying to tell you for the last ten minutes?"

Charley ignored her sarcasm. "Well, at least nothing bad can happen to us in a cartoon," she said, looking on the bright side.

But as she spoke a shadow fell over them.

Lizzie and Charley looked up. The blue and white butterfly on Lizzie's hand looked up too.

"Uh-oh," muttered Charley. "I think I spoke too soon."

Far in the distance, but nonetheless unmistakable, the Wei warship hovered at the edge of the scene, squeezed between the clouds and a dark green hill, casting a long shadow before it.

"At least it's not coming very fast," said the

optimistic Charley.

Indeed, the Wei craft was too big for the Wabbitville sky and could move only slowly through the clouds.

Lizzie refused to be cheered. "But it is coming – sooner or later."

The two girls sat side by side, staring at the dark, looming shape. They might have sat like that until the Wei ship managed to reach them if Flyed hadn't chosen to act. He took one look at the shape above them and decided to go somewhere else. His departure finally tore Lizzie's attention from the Wei ship.

"Flyed!" she shouted. "Flyed, come back!"

"He's heading for that pink and yellow cloud," announced Charley.

"Flyed!" screamed Lizzie. "Flyed, you can't hide in that cloud. It's just a cartoon!"

Flyed, however, had no intention of coming back. He flew swiftly towards the hilltop where the pink and yellow cloud had begun to shimmer, as if it were glad to see him.

Lizzie felt certain that Mrs Moscos was not going to be happy if they lost Flyed in the Wabbits' cartoon.

"Come on!" she shouted. "We have to catch him!"

Charley needed no further prompting. She was on her feet even before Lizzie. "What are you waiting for?" she shrieked. "Let's go!"

The Wabbits looked up from their picnic as Lizzie and Charley raced towards them.

"Who are those girls? What are they doing here?" squealed Wanda Wabbit. And then, in the same breath, asked, "Is that a spaceship?"

"It can't be a spaceship," answered Wilbur. "There aren't any spaceships in Wabbitville."

"Stop that butterfly!" screamed Lizzie. "Don't let him get away!"

But the Wabbits made no move to stop Flyed. He soared over their heads to disappear into the cloud behind them.

Indeed, instead of stopping Flyed, the Wabbits simply stopped. Their faces were frozen in Wabbit surprise as they stared past the girls for almost half a second – and then they turned and ran.

Lizzie's and Charley's eyes met.

"I'm not looking round," said Charley. "I don't want to see how close they are."

Lizzie wasn't about to look round either. In any event, she knew how close the Wei ship was: she could see its shadow edging forward on the ground.

And then, in case there was any doubt about how close the ship was getting, it started to speak.

"This is the Wei warship," said a voice they'd heard before. "Because of the way you keep slipping through space and time, we now believe that one of you must be Flyed, travelling in disguise. If you give yourself up we promise that we will spare your companion. Otherwise you both must die."

Charley glanced at Lizzie. "I don't suppose you'd consider surrendering?"

"I wouldn't even consider surrendering you," answered Lizzie. "It's not as if the Weis are known for keeping their word, is it?"

Charley knew Lizzie was right, but she groaned anyway. "We're doomed, aren't we? No wonder Flyed disguised himself as a butterfly. He can just fly off when things get tough."

Lizzie grabbed hold of Charley's arm. "That's it!" she cried. "That's it!"

Charley didn't look as happy as Lizzie sounded. "What's it?"

"Flyed's found another door!" Still holding on to Charley, Lizzie started to run.

"Oh, you have got to be joking…" gasped Charley as, out of breath, they came to a stop at the shiny red plane.

Uncle Buck's pride and joy was very small, and had silver propellers and a silver key in its tail to make it go.

Lizzie was already turning the silver key. "It's our only chance. Get in!"

"This plane can't go fast enough to escape a Wei warship," protested Charley as she hauled herself over the side.

"It can take us to that cloud, though," said Lizzie. It seemed to her that the most important thing was to find Flyed. If they didn't find Flyed it didn't really matter what else happened.

As soon as the plane was wound up, she scrambled into the cockpit beside Charley. Trying very hard to be calm, she grabbed hold of the steering wheel and pulled back. The plane immediately started to whirr – and then, very slowly, it started to rise.

Charley turned to Lizzie in obvious surprise. "I didn't know you could fly a plane."

Lizzie gripped the wheel with both hands. "Neither did I."

Whirring determinedly, Uncle Buck's plane struggled towards the pink and yellow cloud. But now that they were close to it, Lizzie noticed something about the cloud that she hadn't noticed before. It was shaped like a giant butterfly, dappled with sunlight. The blue and white wings of the great rebel leader beat against its centre like a heart.

"There he is!" shouted Lizzie. "Don't worry, Flyed! We're coming!"

Charley was looking behind them. "Hurry!" she ordered. "Can't you make this thing go any faster?"

"I'm afraid we only have one speed," said Lizzie between clenched teeth. If she hadn't been so busy flying the plane she would have given Charley a poke.

"But they're gain—" Charley broke off with a squeak of alarm. "Oh, no! I see guns!" She turned back to Lizzie and grabbed her by the shoulder. "Do something!" she bellowed. "I see guns!"

It was unclear to Lizzie just what Charley thought she could do. She pressed her foot to the floor, but since Uncle Buck's plane didn't have an accelerator pedal the plane went no faster.

"Go!" Charley urged. "Go! Go! Go!"

For lack of anything more useful to do, Lizzie joined in. "Go! Go! Go!"

They weren't more than a few metres away from Flyed when a missile in a very attractive shade of purple passed them so closely that they could feel its heat.

"Oh, no!" wailed Charley. "We really are doomed!"

All at once there was a mighty roar as dozens of voices started chanting, "No, no, no! Go, go, go! No, no, no! Go, go, go!"

Lizzie remembered her mother saying that, when driving, one should never take one's eyes from the road. She reckoned this rule applied to toy planes as well as cars, so she didn't look round. Charley, however, did.

"It's the little kids watching the cartoon!" she announced. "I can see them. They're standing on their seats."

The crew of the Wei warship also heard the chanting children. Not expecting an audience, they braked in confusion.

"They've stopped!" shouted Charley.

"Go, go, go..." cried the children.

Lizzie screamed, "Flyed! We're coming!" as

loudly as she could and steered the little plane straight into the cloud.

"Hidden at last!" gasped Charley, ready to collapse with relief.

At which words Uncle Buck's red plane turned on its side unexpectedly, dumping Lizzie and Charley into the cloud. From which point they continued down. Down through the sky – and then down right through the ground.

Charley's voice was the only sound to be heard.

"I should have known it was too good to be true," it said.

The Wild, Wild West

Having fallen out of the plane, straight through the cloud, and then through the ground of Wabbitville, Lizzie, Charley and Flyed finally landed in a heap on a haystack that was inconveniently located in the middle of nowhere.

"I'm never going to listen to you again for as long as I live, Lizzie Wesson," said Charley once she'd recovered her breath. She pulled straw from her hair. "Not ever. Every time I listen to you something awful happens. The next time we have tickets for Screen Five, I'm going into Screen Five – not Screen Six."

Lizzie sat up, removing several pieces of straw from her own hair with the hand that wasn't occupied by a sleeping butterfly. "That's gratitude for you," she snapped. "You should be thanking me and Flyed for saving you, not telling me off."

"Saving me?" Charley glared back at her as
ferociously as someone who has just fallen
into a rather foul-smelling haystack can glare.
"You call this being saved?" Charley's laugh
contained some bitterness. "You obviously
haven't noticed, Lizzie, but this isn't exactly
being saved. This is being dumped out of one
disaster and into another. I don't call that
anything like being saved."

"All right," Lizzie conceded, "not exactly
saved. But at least we've been moved."
Careful not to wake Flyed, she got to her feet
for a better look around. "I just wonder
where we've been moved to this time."

Ahead of them lay a vast expanse of
extraordinarily little. Far in the distance were
green mountains, but where Lizzie, Charley
and the great rebel leader found themselves
there were only dry earth, clumps of
sagebrush and cacti, a broken wagon wheel
and the remains of a barn.

"We must be in another film," said Charley.

She pulled some straw from her sleeve and sighed. "But probably not the musical…"

Lizzie gestured to the cacti and the wagon wheel. "It must be the Western." She looked over at Charley. "We can't just stand out here, waiting for the Wei warship to find us. I reckon we'd better go on."

"I suppose so…" Charley got to her feet with a weary sigh. "But where to?"

"There's a road." Lizzie pointed at the narrow trail a few metres away. "Road" might be a slight exaggeration, but at least it seemed to be going somewhere. "And look, I see smoke in the distance. That must be the town. Maybe Mrs Moscos is waiting for us there."

Hunger was making Charley grumpy. "What if it's not the town?" she grumbled. "What if it's an Indian camp?"

"Then I reckon you'll finally learn to ride a horse," said Lizzie, and with that she marched off towards the ribbon of dirt.

It was a narrow trail, but it was a long one.

Lizzie cupped a hand over the sleeping butterfly to protect him from the dust that got in their noses and covered their clothes. Their feet ached. Charley's stomach growled so much that the first time she heard it Lizzie thought it was a wolf and screamed. By the time they finally reached a sign that said WELCOME TO THIS WILL DO, ARIZONA, neither Lizzie nor Charley would have minded if it had been an Indian camp, so long as they could sit down.

"Gosh," said Charley as they slowly approached the two lines of wooden buildings that made up the main street of This Will Do. All the windows had their shutters closed and all the doors were shut tight. "It seems awfully quiet."

"That's just because there's no one here," said Lizzie.

Charley didn't find this particularly comforting. "Do you think it's a ghost town?" she asked nervously.

There was a shrill laugh, and then someone

said, "Not yet, but it will be soon."

Charley and Lizzie looked round. An extremely dirty cowboy had ridden up behind them.

"Afternoon, ladies." The cowboy touched his hat, causing a small cloud of dust to rise into the air. "If you want some advice, you'd best be doing what you see me doing and get out of town before the shootin' starts."

Charley looked at Lizzie. "Shooting?"

"That's right," said the cowboy.

"What sort of shooting?" asked Lizzie.

The cowboy elaborated. "Gunfight. B'tween two of the meanest gangs of outlaws this side of the Mississippi."

"Oh." Lizzie felt that she was getting pretty good at taking bad news in her stride. "Well, we certainly don't want to disturb them. We…" She hesitated. This didn't seem like the right moment to mention that they were being chased by a Wei warship. There wasn't time to even try to explain. "We're just passing through."

The cowboy spat on the ground. "If I were you I wouldn't pass through just yet. I'd find myself some cover and wait till the shooting stops." He grinned. "Shouldn't take long."

"That sounds like an excellent idea to me," said Charley.

But Lizzie had hold of her elbow and was trying to pull her forward. "We don't have time to wait till the shooting stops," hissed Lizzie. "Look over there – at the hotel."

On the other side of the street, square in the middle, stood the hotel. It was the only building in town that didn't have its shutters closed. There were yellowed lace curtains in the windows and a faded sign over the opened door that said THIS WILL DO HOTEL. Standing in front of the door was a very rough-looking man all in black with several rough-looking and heavily armed men on either side of him. None of them looked particularly pleasant.

"Gunslingers!" gasped Charley.

"That gentleman right there has more

notches on his gun than you've had hot dinners," the cowboy informed them. "So if you ladies don't mind, I think I'll be taking my leave about now."

Charley moved as though she wanted to go with him.

Lizzie tugged on her arm. "I didn't mean look at the gunslingers. I meant look up over the roof…"

Charley wasn't sure that she wanted to see something that was worse than a gang of gunslingers, but she took a deep breath and raised her eyes. Above the roof of the hotel and far in the distance – though not far enough – she could just make out the Wei warship breaking through the sky.

"Oh, no," groaned Charley. She turned back to Lizzie. "We'll have to hide in the hotel."

"And how are we going to get over to the hotel?" asked Lizzie. She jerked her head towards the street. "Are you planning to walk through *them*?"

In the few seconds Charley had her eyes on the Wei warship, the unpleasant-looking men had moved to the centre of the main street. There they'd been joined by another gang of men who, if anything, looked even more unpleasant.

"We could go around them," suggested Charley. "Next to the buildings."

Lizzie made a face. "But we'd still get shot."

As desperate to get out of This Will Do as she was, Charley could see that Lizzie had a point.

"Well, what if we asked politely? Maybe they'd let us pass before they start gunning each other down."

Lizzie looked sceptical.

Charley squashed her lips together scornfully. "I suppose you have a better idea?"

Since Lizzie, in fact, did not have a better idea, she took a deep breath and called to the men in the street.

"Excuse me!" Lizzie's voice was loud but polite. "We're very sorry to bother you, but my friend and I were wondering if we could just get across the street before you actually start shooting."

There were a few hoots of laughter from his friends, but the man in black didn't so much as smile.

"Who the heck are you?" he demanded. "What are you two doing in our gunfight?"

"Nothing," Charley quickly assured him. "We wouldn't think of interfering in your gunfight." She held up her hands. "We don't even have guns. If we could just get to the other side of—"

"Go on home! Get out of here!" hollered the man with all the notches on his gun. "And do it pronto!"

"But that's what we want to do," said Lizzie. "We want to get out of here. We want to cross the street."

The gunslinger eyed her suspiciously. "You're not crossing anything," he told her.

"How do I know you're not up to something? It could be some kind of trick."

"Oh, it's not a trick," Lizzie and Charley assured him. "We just want to get to the hotel."

The leader of the second gang yawned loudly. "How long is this going to take?" he demanded. He spat on the ground. "Like as not, you put these two brats up to this, to delay your death by a few more minutes."

"Hogwash," snarled the leader of the first gang. "You're the one who's got the appointment in the cemetery." He too spat on the ground. "We're ready when you are. I ain't waitin' on these two any longer. If they don't want to clear off, then it's their tough jerky."

Carrying on as though Lizzie and Charley had got out of the way as they'd been told, the two groups of men began to walk very slowly backwards, their hands held over their guns. They were watching each other so closely that none of them noticed the darkening sky.

Lizzie, however, had noticed the darkening sky. "Please!" she screamed. "It won't take us more than a few seconds."

"What did I say?" bawled the man in black. "Get outta here! We start shootin' on the count of ten. One … two … three…"

It was on the count of six that the flashing purple lights of the approaching Wei ship fell over them and the earth trembled.

The man in black stopped counting and put his hands on his hips, glaring straight ahead. "Is that an earthquake?" he demanded. "Isn't it enough that we've got little girls running all over town? Now we're having an earthquake. Has somebody changed the script?"

The leader of the second gang, however, was not glaring straight ahead. He was staring above him, his jaw dropping in some surprise. "Jumpingeehosseffers!" he shouted. "What the heck is that?"

The other gunslingers all followed his gaze.

"It looks like a spaceship," said one.

"It can't be," said another. "This is 1853. There aren't any spaceships in 1853."

"Come on!" Lizzie urged in a whisper. "Now's our chance."

Charley was only too happy to obey. Barely daring to breathe, the girls scuttled off the wooden walkway, their hands held so tightly that the knuckles were white. Once in the street, they quickly but cautiously edged their way around the men, who were still staring up at the sky, too bewildered to move.

And they would have made it too. They were directly behind the first gang of gunslingers and halfway to the hotel, when Flyed woke up again.

"Uh-oh," whispered Lizzie as the blue and white wings started to flutter.

Charley looked over just in time to see the great rebel leader launch himself back the way they'd come. There was nothing on the other side of the street but a wooden water trough and, behind that, a row of buildings whose doors were all firmly shut.

"Lizzie, no!" hissed Charley as Lizzie took a step away from the hotel. "There's nowhere to hide over there." She tightened her hold on Lizzie's hand. "We're going to—"

The sentence Charley was trying to say was "We're going to the hotel, remember?" but she never finished it because at that instant Lizzie yanked her hand free and went running after the blue and white butterfly.

There was nothing Charley could do except follow.

Flyed came to a halt directly over the trough of water.

"Now what are we supposed to do?" demanded Charley. "Jump into that?"

"Exactly," said Lizzie. She put her hands on the edge of the trough and started to pull herself up.

"You really are mad, aren't you?" asked Charley. "There is no way I'm getting into that filthy water. It's full of dead insects."

"Oh, for heaven's sake," sighed Lizzie. "You can't let a little thing like that stop you." She pointed into the trough. "Take a good look at the water. Don't you see what else is in it?"

Making a disgusted face, Charley peered into the water. A faint pattern shone on the surface. She shrugged. "So what?"

"So what? Don't you see what it is? It's butterflies!"

"No, it isn't," Charley insisted. "It's just the light from the Wei warship."

Lizzie stared at her. "You don't get it, do you? Think about what happened before – the butterflies on the vision screen ... the butterfly cloud... It's not light from the ship making that pattern, Charley. It's Flyed. Whenever he finds a door through space and time, he makes butterflies appear so we know."

Charley looked at the not-very-clean water in the trough. "Are you telling me that's a door?"

"Yes," said Lizzie. "That's what I'm telling you. Now jump in."

Charley still wasn't sure. It was the Wei warship that made up her mind for her. It moved into position directly overhead.

A huge violet spotlight went on in the belly of the ship and then the ship (or so it seemed) began to speak. "We want Flyed!" bellowed the ship. "And we want him now!"

"I don't believe this, Lizzie Wesson," said Charley as she hauled herself over the edge of the trough. "On top of everything, it will ruin my hair."

No Place Like Home

Neither Lizzie nor Charley was really sure what happened next. One instant there was a splash as they flung themselves into the trough; the next they were standing beside a palm tree, dripping water onto a polished stone floor.

Lizzie examined the great rebel leader of the Ganowans, who was sitting on her hand, to make sure he was sleeping and not drowned. "It's amazing," said Lizzie. "He isn't even wet."

"Well, I am," complained Charley, wringing the hem of her skirt. "And my hair is totally ruined."

"Which is what?" asked Lizzie. "Which is worse than being captured by the Weis?"

"Well, no... If you put it like that..." Charley stopped fussing with her skirt and straightened up. "Good grief!" she cried, almost afraid to trust her own eyes. "Lizzie, do you see where we are? It's the Victoria Shopping Centre!" She grabbed Lizzie's arm and gave it a shake. "Lizzie, we made it! We're back home."

Lizzie tore her attention from Flyed and looked around. "I don't believe it." There wasn't a spaceship, a cartoon animal, a cowboy or, more importantly, a Wei warship in sight. "We really are home!"

Charley collapsed with relief on the bench beside the palm tree. "I could kiss the ground," she announced with great feeling. "I really could."

Lizzie plopped down beside her. "Don't start kissing anything yet," she advised. "We still have to find Mrs Moscos."

Having recovered from her great relief, Charley glanced around. Everything was as it should be, except for one thing: there wasn't another person anywhere in sight. "Where do you think everybody is?" she asked.

Lizzie shrugged. "Dunno." She was so happy to see something as familiar as the local shopping centre that she hadn't noticed there was nobody in it. "Maybe there's a raffle going on or something."

"That'll be it," agreed Charley. "A raffle. Or maybe a puppet show."

Lizzie, however, was now looking around them with a worried look on her face. "There's no one in any of the shops either." She tilted her head to one side, listening for something. "And there isn't any music." There was always music playing in the Victoria Shopping Centre.

"Well maybe the sound system's broken," said Charley absent-mindedly. Now that they weren't being pursued by the Wei army and could relax a bit, she was rummaging through her pockets in the hopes of finding a forgotten sweet or a piece of chocolate.

"So why isn't anyone in any of the shops?" persisted Lizzie. Unless you counted the mannequins in the windows, which Lizzie wasn't counting, there was nothing even vaguely human except for her and Charley to be seen.

Charley shook out one of her pockets. Several bits of paper drifted to the floor. "How should I know? Maybe it's a big lottery draw. You know, for millions of pounds or something."

That would explain why there was no music and no one in the shops.

Lizzie frowned. "Can you hear helicopters?" she asked.

Charley stuffed her pocket back in place and jumped to her feet. "Give me a break, will you, Lizzie? We're all right. We made it back safe and sound. Stop looking for trouble."

Lizzie may have been looking for trouble, but she wasn't looking at Charley. She was gazing up at the glass dome that covered the plaza of the Victoria Shopping Centre.

"Well, can you hear helicopters?" Lizzie asked again.

Charley sighed mightily, making a big production of looking up at the ceiling and straining her ears to hear.

"Yes," she finally decided. "Yes, I can hear helicopters." Her tone became sarcastic. "They use them to report the traffic, remember?"

"More than one?" asked Lizzie.

Charley blinked. "More than one…" she repeated, but this time it wasn't a question. "I can hear more than one helicopter," she muttered. "At least three or four."

"Charley," said Lizzie, standing up and taking her arm. "Charley, what were the other films showing in the cinema complex? There was the Western … the cartoon … *Galaxy at War IV*…"

"The thriller." Charley's voice was rather faint. She turned to Lizzie, her face whiter than unbuttered popcorn. "Oh, Lizzie … you don't think…"

"Terrorists love shopping centres," answered Lizzie with the authority of someone who has watched her share of thrillers. "It all makes sense – the empty shops, the lack of music..."

Charley let out a low moan. "Oh, where is Mrs Moscos? Why is she never around when we need her?"

"Forget Mrs Moscos," advised Lizzie. "We've got to get out of here. Quickly."

She cupped a protective hand around Flyed, and then, illustrating what she meant, Lizzie started to run. Charley followed.

They skidded to a halt at the shoe shop at the end of the row. "There should be an exit round this corner," guessed Lizzie.

Cautiously, Lizzie and Charley poked their heads round the corner.

Charley immediately ducked back. "Oh my gosh!" she wailed. "We're surrounded!" She held Lizzie's arm so tightly it felt as though she were trying to pull it off. "We're surrounded by terrorists!"

Lizzie was still peeking round the corner, watching the activity behind the glass door at the end of the next concourse. "They're not terrorists," she reported.

Charley gasped. "What? What do you mean they're not terrorists?"

"Well, not unless they're disguised as the American army and the Los Angeles police," said Lizzie.

Charley's head popped round the corner again. Beyond the glass doors were dozens of police cars and vans bearing the insignia of the Los Angeles Police Department, as well as a fleet of army trucks. It was easy enough to tell the soldiers from the police: the soldiers were in combat fatigues and the police in riot gear.

Charley retreated again, leaning against the wall of the shoe shop. "I don't believe it – this isn't the Victoria Shopping Centre!" Her voice took on a slightly hysterical edge. "But it looks just like it."

Lizzie pulled back too and fell into place beside her. "I suppose shopping centres are like chips," she said. "You know, seen one and you've more or less seen them all."

"Wait a minute!" A sudden smile brightened Charley's face. "This is good news, not bad news, isn't it? I mean, if it's the army and the police that are surrounding the shopping centre then—"

"Then where are the terrorists?" asked Lizzie.

The eerie silence of the mall pressed down on them.

"They're in here, aren't they?" asked Charley in a hoarse whisper. "That's why we're surrounded."

"Don't tell me," said Lizzie. "You've seen this film before."

But if Charley had seen this film before, she probably wouldn't have jumped and screamed the way she did when a stern voice suddenly boomed, "There is no escape! You have ten minutes to release your hostages. If you do not release your hostages within ten minutes, we're coming in!"

"Oh, no!" wailed Charley. "Just when we

thought we were safe."

"Maybe it's not as bad as we think," suggested Lizzie. "You know, maybe we're at the end of the film and the terrorists are ready to give up."

But the words were hardly out of her mouth when the sound system crackled back into life.

"Don't give us ultimatums!" a different voice – presumably one of the terrorists – shouted back. "You have five minutes to meet our demands. If you don't, there won't be any hostages left to worry about."

"Maybe we're the ones who should give up," suggested Charley. "Maybe if we find something to use as a white flag, the police and the army will let us out without shooting us first."

Lizzie fidgeted with indecision. "I don't know… What if they think we're trying to trick them, like the gunslingers did? Or what if the terrorists see us and shoot us to stop us from getting away?" She looked down at the blue and white butterfly gently twitching on her forearm. "What do you think, Flyed? What would you do?"

Great rebel leader that he was, Flyed did not fidget with indecision. His answer was swift and certain. He flew away.

"Oh, I don't believe this. Here we go again." Charley was flushed with exasperation as well as anger. "You had to ask him, didn't you? You just had to ask—"

Lizzie grabbed her arm and started to run. "Come on. Flyed always finds the door."

Flyed turned sharp left into the south-east concourse, and Lizzie and Charley turned sharp left after him, stopping so abruptly when they saw what was waiting for them in the south-east concourse that they nearly toppled over.

"Oh, no!" gasped Lizzie. This time, Flyed hadn't found the door. "He's found the terrorists."

Indeed, there were two heavily armed men, their faces hidden by black masks, just outside the travel agent's, guarding the door. Inside the travel agent's were several more terrorists, and at least a hundred shoppers, all of them handcuffed together.

"This is just great," Charley muttered. "He brought us straight to them."

"Halt!" shouted one of the terrorists. "Don't anybody move."

Considering the fact that they had already halted, Lizzie didn't think this caution was really necessary.

On the other hand, perhaps it was.

Flyed fluttered forward.

"Please," said Lizzie, hoping she didn't sound as terrified as she felt. "Don't point that thing at us. Someone might get hurt."

The terrorist leered in a menacing way. "Very perceptive," he said sarcastically. "You must be right at the top of your class."

The other terrorist, however, was looking confused. "Who are these kids?" he wanted to know. "Where did they come from?"

Flyed flew a few centimetres closer to the

men, Lizzie and Charley shuffling after him.

"Didn't you hear me?" asked the first terrorist, waving his rifle back and forth. "Don't anybody move."

"Do you think they're hostages?" asked the second man.

His comrade laughed. "Well, they aren't the army."

"No," Lizzie quickly agreed. "No, we're not the army. And we're not the police either."

"But if they're hostages," said the second terrorist, "then how did they get out here?"

Something clicked very ominously.

Lizzie tried to ignore the sound. Still following Flyed, she edged forward.

"Lizzie, please…" Charley tugged at her arm. "Don't go any closer. They're going to shoot us!"

As if agreeing with Charley, the first guard shouted, "I'm warning you! Don't come any closer."

Lizzie's eyes were on Flyed. Slowly but

surely, he rose in the air, until he was over the heads of the guards. But Flyed wasn't the only thing that was over the heads of the guards.

"I don't think you are going to shoot us," said Lizzie. She almost felt like smiling. "I think you'll be too busy for that."

The terrorists laughed. "Oh, really? And what are we supposed to be busy with?"

It was the shopping centre's sound system that answered this question.

"This is a Wei warship," announced the now familiar voice. "You have thirty of your Earth seconds to put down your weapons and hand over the great rebel leader Flyed or we're coming in to get him." Instantly, the voice began to count down. "Thirty ... twenty-nine ..."

Instead of looking up, which would have given them an excellent view of the Wei warship hovering overhead, the terrorists continued to look at Lizzie and Charley.

"Did he say 'fly up' or 'fried'?" asked the first man.

"What was that?" asked the second.

"He didn't say either," said Lizzie. "He said *Flyed*." She pointed to the glass roof above them. "And that," she said, "is the Wei warship."

The terrorists gazed upwards in very sincere astonishment.

"… twenty-two … twenty-one …"

"Barking bayonets," muttered one. "That's not an army helicopter."

The other turned back to Charley and Lizzie. "Then one of you must be this Fly character."

This was so obviously not a statement but a threat that Charley, caught by surprise, blurted out, "No, it isn't one of us! Flyed's the butterfly."

"… seventeen … sixteen …"

What with all the things they had to take in – the police … the army … the Wei warship – neither of the terrorists had noticed the butterfly, now fluttering gracefully past them.

"What butterfly?" asked the first terrorist.

The second terrorist nudged him with the butt of his gun. "She must mean that butterfly," he said, and moved the barrel of his rifle so that it pointed at the blue and white wings hovering just above the rubbish bin in the middle of the concourse.

"… ten … nine …"

The other man laughed uneasily, but looked back at Lizzie and Charley. "Are you saying that … that whatever it is up there wants this butterfly?"

"Well—" began Charley, but Lizzie stepped on her foot and she didn't go on.

"Well, let them have it, that's what I say!" suggested terrorist number one.

"Oh, no!" cried Charley and Lizzie. "You can't do that! You—"

"Oh yes we can." In no mood for an argument, the terrorists turned their weapons on the blue and white butterfly as it hovered above the rubbish bin. "Just watch."

But the butterfly had vanished inside the bin.

"… eight … seven …"

The terrorists reacted quickly. They turned their rifles on Lizzie and Charley. "Go get him!" they ordered.

It was rare for Lizzie to be happy to do what she was told, but she was very happy now.

"Of course," she said, pulling Charley after her. "We'll have him right out."

"Oh, Lizzie, be reasonable," moaned Charley. "It's full of rubbish. Are you sure he's gone in there?"

"Yes." Lizzie climbed up on the bench beside the bin, still pulling Charley after her. "I'm absolutely positive."

"Oi!" shouted one of the men. "What are you doing? Just dump everything on the floor."

"Oh, we don't want to make a mess," Lizzie called back.

Charley gazed down at the mound of empty paper cups and burger boxes. "Not only is it disgusting, but there's no way we're going to fit in there."

"… four … three … two …"

The first terrorist was looking up at the Wei warship. "Hold on!" he shouted. "We're getting him for you! Hold on!"

"Hurry!" hissed Lizzie and she scrabbled over the side of the bin.

Charley hurried. She took a deep breath, held her nose and pitched herself over the rim.

The last thing the terrorists heard Charley say was, "I'm warning you, Lizzie Wesson. If this skirt gets stained I am never ever going to forgive you."

And then the voice from the Wei warship said, "One."

Singing in the Train

Lizzie and Charley landed with a gentle thump in the only two empty seats in a crowded railway carriage. There were sweet wrappers and crisp packets hanging off their clothes, but otherwise the journey through the rubbish bin had left them unharmed – or almost.

"I knew it!" Charley rubbed at the ketchup stain she'd just discovered on her skirt. "Didn't I tell you this would happen? My mother will kill me if this doesn't come out."

"That's the least of our problems," answered Lizzie.

There was something in her voice that made Charley stop fretting about her skirt and look up. Lizzie was frantically rummaging through the empty wrappers on the floor.

"What's wrong?" asked Charley.

"We've lost Flyed. He usually lands on me, but I can't find him anywhere." Lizzie sat back in her seat with a groan. Mrs Moscos was going to blame her for this.

Mrs Moscos wasn't the only one.

"What do you mean you've lost him?" Charley's voice was shrill. "You can't have lost him. You said you saw him go into the bin."

"I did see him go into the bin," snapped Lizzie. "But it doesn't look like he came back out."

Charley scowled. "I should have known something like this would happen. First you make me leap into a galaxy; then you make me fly into a cloud; then you nearly get me drowned; then you make me jump into a revolting rubbish bin – and now this! We're never going to get home, and I'm already feeling weak with hunger."

Lizzie wasn't listening. It occurred to her that Mrs Moscos might be on the train. That would explain why Flyed wasn't with Lizzie and Charley: he was with Mrs Moscos. Lizzie's eyes searched the crowded carriage.

The train they were on was an old-fashioned one that chugged along under a cloud of black smoke. It was filled with women in long skirts and bonnets and men in stiff suits and narrow-brimmed hats; there was no one wearing a blonde wig and the blue and white uniform of the Ganowan army with a butterfly on her shoulder.

Seeing Lizzie searching the carriage, Charley too turned her attention to their fellow travellers. "Where do you think we are?" she asked. "Everybody looks so weird."

"We're in the nineteenth century," said Lizzie airily. Much to her own amazement, she recognized the style of dress of the other passengers from the historical dramas her mother liked to watch on TV.

Charley's stomach rumbled. "Do you suppose they had buffet cars in the nineteenth century?" she asked.

Lizzie started to say that it was more important to find the next door through time and space than the snack bar when the young woman two rows in front of them unexpectedly got to her feet and burst into song.

"Oh, my," said Charley. "I do believe we're in the musical."

Lizzie was staring at the young woman and didn't hear Charley. The young woman had the same ginger hair as Lizzie herself and, on her left shoulder, an unusual brooch in the shape of a butterfly.

"Charley," hissed Lizzie. "Charley, look at her dress."

"Good grief … it's…" Charley rubbed her eyes as though they might be misleading her. "It's Flyed!"

"He must have mistaken her for me because of the hair," Lizzie reasoned.

Displaying a depressing lack of confidence in her friend, Charley said, "I don't suppose you have a plan for getting him back, then?"

"As a matter of fact, I do." Lizzie was quite proud that she had come up with an idea so quickly, especially one that was simple and entailed no danger. All they had to do was wait until the young woman finished her song and then they would ask for their butterfly back.

It was quite a long song about the young woman's love for a highwayman. By the time it began to draw to a close, Charley was nodding off.

"Wake up!" Lizzie jabbed her in the ribs. "It's almost over."

Lizzie stood up, ready to carry out her simple plan.

But plans – even simple ones – don't always go the way they should. It was at this very moment that Lizzie's plan began to go wrong. As the young woman's song ended, the train screeched to a halt.

The other passengers immediately leapt to their feet and started dashing about, waving their arms and gasping. Several of them were looking out the windows, craning their necks to see down the side of the train. "What happened?" they asked one another in sing-song voices. "What on earth could be wrong?"

"Oh, no, now what?" wailed Charley.

Almost instantly her question was answered.

"Brigands!" shouted someone at the back. "Brigands have stopped the train!"

"This is all we need," wailed Lizzie. There was no way they could ask for their butterfly back in all this confusion.

The people around them picked up the chant. "Brigands! Brigands! What shall we do? Oh, what shall we do?"

"Big what?" asked Charley, pressing her face to the window for a look.

"Brigands," answered Lizzie. "You know, highwaymen – like Dick Turpin. It must be the hero."

"Lizzie," said Charley. "Lizzie, those aren't brigands out there. And I don't reckon they're heroes either."

Lizzie was too worried about Flyed to pay much attention to what Charley was saying. "Why not?"

"Because they're wearing capes," reported Charley.

"Highwaymen wore capes."

Charley looked back at her. "With silver linings?"

"The Weis!" The other passengers were all standing in the aisle, trying to see what was going on, so there was no point in trying to get to the front of the carriage that way. Lizzie started scrabbling over the next seat. "Come on, we have to get Flyed!"

For his part, Flyed had finally woken up and realized his mistake. Which was when he made another: he fluttered his wings.

Despite the general hubbub in the carriage, the young woman noticed that there was something near her shoulder that moved. More than that, because of the dark cloud above them, she could see that whatever it was was glowing as well.

Lizzie's fingers were only inches away from Flyed when the singer let out a shriek and whacked the butterfly from her dress.

"Oh, no!" Lizzie lunged forward. She was not much better at sport than Charley, but she managed to catch Flyed in her outstretched hand.

"Thank heavens for that," breathed Charley.

But although Flyed was still glowing, he was lying very still. Lizzie could tell that, for once, he wasn't asleep.

"Let's not panic," said Lizzie, as much to herself as to Charley. "Maybe he's only stunned." She touched him very gently with the tip of her finger. "Flyed?" she whispered. "Flyed, are you all right?"

Flyed didn't stir.

"Lizzie?" Charley's nails dug into her arm. "Lizzie, I think I'm starting to panic."

Lizzie looked up as the door at the front of the carriage burst open and a Wei soldier marched in, knocking several people back in their seats.

"Duck before he sees you!" ordered Lizzie.

This turned out to be an unnecessary precaution. The Wei soldier wasn't given a chance to see them. Although the pretty young woman was a little taken aback by the sight of him, she determinedly stuck to her script. Flinging herself at the Wei soldier as if he were a handsome highwayman, she burst into song once more.

"This is our chance," decided Lizzie. "We'll sneak out while she's singing to him. If we can find somewhere to hide until the Weis have gone, maybe Flyed will revive enough to find the next door through time and space."

Climbing over sixteen rows proved to be a bit harder than climbing over one row had been. By the time they reached the back of the carriage they were both out of breath.

"I feel like I've been jumping hurdles," gasped Charley. "I do hope the next carriage isn't so crowded."

"It won't be." Lizzie turned the brass knob.

Lizzie was right. The next carriage wasn't nearly as crowded as the previous one. In fact, it wasn't crowded at all. The next carriage wasn't there.

In its place was a very small platform with a rail around it, and behind that the gleaming track and an enormous cloud in the distance that filled up the sky.

"Oh, no…" Charley sounded ready to cry. "And how are we going to find somewhere to hide when there isn't any more train?"

Lizzie looked back at her. "I thought I told you not to—"

Charley's eyes widened. "They're behind us, aren't they? I can tell by the way your mouth is hanging open."

"There's only two," said Lizzie. "They're having trouble getting past the singer and the other Wei."

"Oh, no," wailed Charley. "There's nowhere left to go."

After today, Lizzie was never going to

complain about being bored again. Not ever. That was, of course, assuming that there was a day after today.

"But there is somewhere left to go," said Lizzie desperately. "There's the next door."

"Oh, well that's all right, then," answered Charley. Her eyes went to the limp butterfly on Lizzie's shoulder. "What was I worried about?"

Lizzie saw Charley glance at Flyed. "We'll just have to find it ourselves," said Lizzie. "Mrs Moscos said that every moment has an exit, so this moment must have one too."

"Right," agreed Charley. "Only we don't know where it is. For all we know, it's back inside the train. Do you want to go back inside the train?"

Lizzie admitted that she didn't want to go back inside the train. "But we have to go somewhere. We can't just stand here, waiting to be caught."

Charley held up a hand. "Shhh..." she said softly. "What's that booing?" She peered round Lizzie. "It seems to be coming from out there."

Lizzie turned to look too. Much to her surprise, the entire audience of the musical was hissing, whistling and shouting insults at the screen.

"Good grief!" gasped Lizzie. "They really are booing! They must be upset that the story's changed."

"Your sister looks more than upset," said Charley. "She looks positively livid."

Lizzie followed Charley's gaze to the very front row of the cinema. Allie and Gemma were sitting in the middle, their faces red from screaming.

"What happened to the music?" Allie was shrieking. "Bring back the brigands! This film stinks!"

If their situation had been a little less grim, Lizzie would have laughed out loud. At last Allie was having a terrible time. Lizzie couldn't think of anyone who deserved it more.

Allie, however, could. At that moment she spotted Lizzie and Charley on the observation deck. Instantly, she stood up on her chair and began to shout even more loudly than before. "Lizzie Wesson!" roared Allie. "What are you doing at the back of that train? Get out of there this minute!"

"Tell her to shut up before the Weis hear her," hissed Charley.

It was, however, already too late. The Wei soldiers had heard Allie and were all rushing towards the last carriage.

"They're coming for you, Lizzie," her sister was screaming. "You might as well surrender!"

"Surrender! Surrender!" echoed Gemma. "Surrender! Surrender!"

Charley was looking through the door with the fascination of someone watching her house burn down. One of the Wei soldiers had solved the problem of the singing young woman blocking his way. He had picked her up and thrown her over his shoulder, and was

marching up the aisle, shoving passengers out
of his way. There were several more soldiers
behind him.

"Maybe Allie and Gemma are right," said
Charley. "Maybe we should surrender."

Lizzie had never done anything her sister
told her to do and she wasn't about to change
the habit of a lifetime now. Not bothering to
think, she grabbed hold of Charley and
pushed her sideways. "Up!" she urged.
"Charley, go up!"

"Up?"

Lizzie steered her to the left. "There's a
ladder over there. We can get to the roof."

"That's not a ladder," protested Charley.
"That's just some pegs stuck in the end of the
carriage."

"You're in real trouble now!" screamed Allie.

"Surrender! Surrender!" chanted Gemma.

"Go up!" repeated Lizzie, and she gave
Charley such a shove that if she hadn't gone
up the pegs she would have gone over the
rail.

Huffing and puffing, Charley scrambled up the side of the train, Lizzie at her heels.

"Mrs Limet wouldn't believe her eyes if she saw me now," Charley grunted as she reached the roof. Mrs Limet was her PE teacher. "Mrs Limet thinks—"

Lizzie was never to learn what it was Mrs Limet thought. Charley broke off as her head rose above the roof.

Her next words were, "Good grief, Lizzie. It's Mrs Moscos!"

Everything that Goes Round, Comes Round

Mrs Moscos had landed Uncle Buck's plane on the roof of the train, and was just climbing out of it as Lizzie and Charley scrabbled from the ladder.

"Oh, Mrs Moscos!" they cried, rushing towards her. "We thought you'd never come!"

Mrs Moscos glared at them from under her wig. "And why is that?" she demanded. "Did I not say I would find you? Ganow is not around the next corner, you know. Fortunately, you two kept the Weis busy enough so that I was able to leave the asteroid without too much interference, but these things do take time nevertheless."

The smile on Lizzie's face turned to a look of indignation. "You mean you knew they were going to follow us? You deliberately let them do it?"

"Oh, Mrs Moscos wouldn't do that, would you, Mrs Moscos?" protested Charley. "We've had such a horrible time – terrorists … gunslingers … rubbish…"

Mrs Moscos, however, had little interest in terrorists, gunslingers or rubbish. She decided to change the subject. "Where is Flyed?" she demanded. "You haven't lost him, have you?"

"Of course we haven't lost him." Lizzie was rather relieved that that, at least, was true. "He's right here." She indicated her shoulder. "He's—"

"Sleeping," put in Charley.

"That just shows what two thousand years of guerrilla warfare can do, doesn't it?" commented Mrs Moscos. "The ability to sleep anywhere." Her eyes narrowed. "He looks a little flat." She pursed her lips. "Don't tell me one of you trod on the great rebel leader of the Ganowans?"

"It wasn't us!" said Lizzie and Charley together. "It was the singer. She thought he was a bug and she hit—"

Mrs Moscos held up her hand like a traffic policeman. "Enough! Enough! There is no time for your excuses. You must escape with Flyed before the battle begins."

"What battle?" asked Lizzie. It didn't seem to her that a fight between Mrs Moscos and a troop of Wei soldiers could be considered a battle. Surely a battle had to last for more than half a second.

Mrs Moscos gave her a critical look. "Lizzie Wesson, I don't want to have to mention your negative thinking again. I am more than capable of taking on the Weis single-handedly if I have to. On this occasion, however, it will not be necessary." She gazed over their heads. "This time I have the greatest rebel army in the universe to help me."

Lizzie and Charley followed Mrs Moscos's gaze. Emerging from the enormous cloud behind the train were hundreds of small blue and white spacecraft.

"The Ganowans!" gasped Lizzie.

"Precisely." Mrs Moscos grabbed them both and started shoving them towards the plane. "Now get in and get going."

"But where are we meant to go?" asked Lizzie as she and Charley obediently climbed aboard.

"Where do you think? Disneyland?" Mrs Moscos treated them to one of her louder and more painful sighs. "The peace conference, of course. You have only a few minutes to get Flyed there before the Ganowans are blamed for everything and the universe is plunged into another senseless war."

Lizzie, however, had thought of another obstacle. "But, Mrs Moscos, we can't wake Flyed. How are we meant to find the door?"

"Of course you can't wake Flyed," snapped Mrs Moscos. "As well as being treated like a basketball, he is exhausted. He must conserve his energy so that he can transform himself back when he gets to the conference."

All the while she was talking, Mrs Moscos had been busily winding up the plane. Now she stepped back and waved her hand vaguely towards the east. "Follow that road," she directed. "It will take you to the nearest village."

"And what do we do when we get there?" asked Charley.

"I trust you will have the sense to know that when the time comes," said Mrs Moscos, with a wave of farewell.

The tiny plane whirred and pitched as Lizzie steered it away from the setting sun. The road was right where it was meant to be, and before long a distant church spire rose from the trees.

"We're going to make it," said Lizzie. She felt rather pleased with herself.

"Thank goodness," sighed Charley. "If I don't get something to eat very soon, I'm going to faint." She leaned her head out of the plane and sniffed. "We're getting close.

I smell bread."

Lizzie laughed. "At last your stomach's being useful."

But Charley didn't laugh along. She was still sniffing the air. "There's something else." She sounded puzzled. "I can't quite place it…"

Lizzie's nose twitched. She could smell it too. It was something that didn't belong in the nineteenth century any more than they did.

"It almost smells like petrol," said Lizzie. "But where would petrol come from way back then?"

Because Charley was hanging over the side of the plane, trying to locate the source of the smell, she was able to answer Lizzie's question with some authority. "Probably from a Wei warship." She said it very softly.

Lizzie glanced over as the little plane took another bump. "What Wei warship?"

"The one behind us."

Lizzie looked over her shoulder. Bearing

down on them was the now familiar sight of an armed Wei craft in hot pursuit. "Oh," said Lizzie. "That Wei warship."

Charley sat back in her seat with an unhappy sigh. "I should have known it was too good to be true. We'll never get home now. And we're having pasta for supper and all."

Disaster, however, was making Lizzie more philosophical than usual. "Well, they haven't caught us yet," she pointed out. "They're having trouble flying this low."

Uncle Buck's little plane only just managed to clear the treetops, but now Lizzie brought it down even lower so that they were flying between the rows of trees that lined the road.

Something very bright, very purple and very shrill hit the ground just behind them.

This time it was Charley who looked round. "They're firing at us!" she shrieked.

Lizzie peered over the steering wheel. "It looks like we're coming to the top of a hill. Maybe we can get even lower."

Charley turned round. She could see the point where the road bent downwards.

Lizzie opened her mouth to say, "Didn't I tell you?" but the words froze with terror in her throat as they reached the top of the hill. A velvet wing brushed her cheek, but she was too shocked to notice.

"There's nothing there!" gasped Charley.

Nor was there anything below them. No trees, no road – just a deep blackness that stretched on for ever. Two more Wei missiles shot past them, only to vanish in the blackness as though swallowed by the sea.

That took care of Plan A.

Lizzie moaned. "I don't know what to do."

If they went into the blackness there would be no turning back. Purple light exploded above them. On the other hand, they obviously couldn't stay where they were.

This time, Lizzie felt the wing against her skin. She looked at her shoulder. Flyed was wide awake, ready for take-off. Suddenly she knew exactly what to do.

"Flyed says go," said Lizzie and she pressed forward on the wheel.

"Oh, Lizzie!" wailed Charley as they started to drop. "I hope you know what you're doing, for a change."

The blackness enclosed them like a tunnel. Down ... down ... down ... went the small red plane, the Wei warship right behind it. Down ... down ... down...

And then, just when they thought they would never come to the end, a dazzle of blue and white lights shone straight ahead of them.

"Good grief!" yelped Lizzie. "It's Mrs Moscos's tree."

Now they knew exactly which neutral planet was being used for the peace conference.

Another Wei missile exploded nearby.

The butterfly on Lizzie's shoulder rose in the air. "And this, my friends," said a gentle voice, "is where I get off." And at once the blue and white butterfly changed back into the great rebel leader of Ganow.

Lizzie was no longer paying the slightest bit of attention to where she was going. Her eyes were on Flyed in his blue and white uniform, striding through the air. She was sure she heard cheering as he vanished into the thousands of blue and white fairy lights, shining like stars.

Allie and Gemma were waiting in the lobby for them when they came out of the cinema. Allie and Gemma were tapping their feet and looking at their watches.

Allie started in as soon as she saw them. "What on earth kept you two so long? We've been waiting ages."

"It wasn't anything on Earth," said Charley.

Lizzie gave her a poke. After what happened when Lizzie told her family the truth about going to Wei she wasn't about to repeat the mistake. If Allie and Gemma didn't remember seeing Lizzie and Charley in their film, then that was fine with her.

"It was a long movie," said Lizzie. "It's only just ended."

"That's not true," purred Gemma with one of her sickly smiles. "Everyone else must have left long ago, because you're the only ones who've come out in at least ten minutes."

"Twenty," amended Allie.

They took the bus home in silence.

That is, Lizzie and Charley were silent. Allie and Gemma did nothing but talk about the musical. *Weren't the songs brilliant? Weren't the costumes brilliant? Wouldn't it be brilliant if there were still handsome brigands roaming the highways?*

"I don't get it," whispered Charley. "We saw them booing – and we know they saw us. Why don't they know what happened?"

"I reckon they've forgotten," said Lizzie. "Mrs Moscos must've used her memory eraser on them. Like she will with us."

Charley sighed. "I suppose it's for the best. Nobody would believe us anyway."

While everyone was watching television

that night, Lizzie slipped from the house and into the garden. There were one or two things she wanted to discuss with Mrs Moscos before she did forget what had happened.

Mrs Moscos was up in her tree again.

"You're not taking down the lights, are you?" asked Lizzie.

"And why shouldn't I be taking down the lights?" asked Mrs Moscos. "I believe they are not needed any more."

"You mean because we got Flyed safely to the peace conference?" asked Lizzie.

Mrs Moscos wrapped another strand of light round her like a necklace. "Flyed? Peace conference? What are you talking about now, Lizzie Wesson?"

"You know," insisted Lizzie, "Flyed, the great rebel leader of the planet Ganow. Louis Wu was trying to kill him, and Charley and I helped him escape. And then the Wei army was after us, but we got Flyed to the peace conference on time and ruined

Louis Wu's plans."

Mrs Moscos's eyebrow rose. "It wouldn't happen to be a science fiction movie you saw this afternoon, would it?"

"Well, yes," said Lizzie. "But…"

"Then I think you are letting your imagination carry you far away," judged Mrs Moscos.

"No, I'm not. Charley and I were in all the movies showing at the cinema today. And you were there too. You were in the musical. Allie and Gemma even saw us."

Mrs Moscos lowered herself onto the wall with remarkable agility for a woman her age. "Allie and Gemma saw no such thing," she informed Lizzie coolly.

"But they did! They even told us to surrender."

"It certainly doesn't look as if it's advice you took, does it?" Mrs Moscos began removing rows of lights from round her neck and putting them on the wall in a way that suggested their conversation was at an end.

So much for asking Mrs Moscos questions.

"But—"

"If I were you, I should go straight to bed and get a good night's sleep," said Mrs Moscos. She jumped down into her garden, wearing her lights like bracelets now. "You're obviously exhausted. I'm sure you'll feel much better in the morning."

Lizzie pulled herself up on the wall to watch her go back to her house.

"But Mrs Moscos!" she called. "I had things I wanted to ask you!"

Mrs Moscos opened her back door. "You may ask me in the morning." She turned round. It was getting dark, and the blue and white lights seemed almost to glow. "And Lizzie," said Mrs Moscos, "that was very clever of you to work out about the butterflies and the doors."

And with that she marched inside.